International Standard Book Number 13:
Hardback 978-1-60452-199-3
Softback 978-1-60452- 200-6
eBook 978-1-60452- 201-3

International Standard Book Number 10:
Hardback 1-60452-199-6
Softback 1-60452-200-3
eBook 1-60452-201-1

Library of Congress Control Number: 2024940535

BluewaterPress LLC
1218 Willow Oak Dr
Edgewater, Florida 32132

http://www.bluewaterpress.com

CHARLIE STANEK'S WAR

by

Robert Tecklenburg

Those who make peaceful revolution impossible will make violent revolution inevitable

--John F. Kennedy

Chapter 1

Explosions punctuated by the rat-tat-tat of gunfire shook the midnight quiet. Sirens screamed into the darkness. Young and old ran into the narrow streets half-asleep as the Cho Lon District of Saigon erupted in violence not experienced since the war with the French.

The headquarters of the Vietnam National Army had come under sudden attack from the Binh Xuyen sect, a powerful crime syndicate that dominated local politics. With an estimated 40,000 armed men under his command, Binh Xuyen's leader, Bay Vien, was a force in South Vietnam. The attack on army headquarters told President Bao Dai and Prime Minister Ngo Dinh Diem that they had run out of peaceful options. They now had to deal with the gangster another way.

Bay Vien ran his crime operation from Le Grand Monde gambling casino in the heart of the city. President Bao Dai had given him full authority over the national police, but Prime Minister Diem later abruptly removed the chief of police from Bay Vien's control, then ordered him to surrender and place his army under the full control of the state. The order sparked a violent reaction from Bay Vien, who ordered the attack on the National Army's Saigon headquarters.

Earlier in the month, with two other South Vietnamese sects—Cao Dai and Hoa Hao, the Binh Xuyen formed a National Front to confront Diem with their demand that the government establish a "national union" to include them. The French Army, having not yet pulled its forces from Indochina, threw its support to this National Front. They believed Diem, an aristocrat and notorious playboy, had little empathy or even understanding for the Vietnamese peasants who composed about 90 percent of the population. Not that they cared for the poor. It was all about power and control.

Diem, of course, refused the demands of the National Front, and included a counter-demand that Binh Xuyen evacuate buildings and areas under their control in Saigon.

Bay Vien refused Diem's ultimatum to submit. Under cover of darkness, his men attacked the army compound near the Chinese district of Saigon. Their infantry assaulted the gates and barricades erected around the perimeter following a brief mortar barrage. Vietnamese Rangers met the attackers with short violent clashes erupting near the front gate.

The brief battle swayed back and forth, but was inconclusive. The Binh Xuyen soldiers finally withdrew before sunrise, leaving 10 of their number dead on the streets. The Army lost six. Bodies of civilians caught in the crossfire littered the streets surrounding the compound.

American Military Mission Headquarters, Binh Hoa, March 29, 1955: "Sir, Diem has to go. He's out of touch with the peasants. There is open rebellion against him. Look! You can still see the smoke from the fighting last night," Colonel Edward Archer, Assistant Air Attaché and head of the American's CIA Military

Mission, urged his commanding officer, General Lawton Stone, heading up the American Mission in South Vietnam.

General Stone seriously considered Archer's assessment. "The Secretary of State is quickly losing confidence in Diem. He says, 'Seek out a replacement now among the various political groups,'" Stone replied, waving the telegram from Washington. "He's certainly changed his mind from a month ago."

"It's about time. We're on the verge of civil war here," Archer growled at the top of his lungs. He paced the room like an angry dog—back and forth, back and forth. "We have to find someone, anyone who can unite this country against the Communists and the other factions. Hell, they all got their own private armies like this Binh Xuyen sect."

"But who?" Stone asked. "Most have close ties to the North, are corrupt, or out of touch. What of the French? They know the politics here much better than we."

"They heavily supported the sects during their war, and have no respect for the Bao Dai Government," the colonel replied. "Things are changing here fast and the French are focused on pulling their troops out. Their war is over."

"General Ely has advised me that by July 1, France will turn over all control of the National Army to the government of Vietnam," Stone said. "I can consult with him to find a suitable replacement for Diem."

"The French?" he asked. "Is that wise?"

"You have another idea, Colonel?"

"I know one person who could advise us. She served with the Viet Minh, but also has ties to politicians here in Saigon, and is even related to Bao Dai," Archer said. "She hates the French, but most importantly, she owns an established business here. That's why she has stayed in the South. If she fled north, her world, but especially her lifestyle would change dramatically. May I add that she is part owner in the Grand Monde Casino? She would have a lot to lose if it were closed or destroyed."

"Good motivation to broker a peace between the sects and the government, or at the very least, suggest a suitable replacement for the Prime Minister," Stone said. "What's her name?"

"She goes by Madame Thieu and is well-known in Saigon."

The general listened quietly. "No grand casinos, villa with servants, or trips to Manila or Paris if she were in Hanoi under the Communists, eh? She doesn't sound too committed then, or should I say she's very pragmatic? Will she trust us? That's an important question, I think."

Archer shrugged. "No more than we can trust her."

"That's a good way to see it, Colonel."

"In Vietnam, it is better and safer to trust no one."

"Meet with her. What do we have to lose?"

"There is a serious drawback to using this woman, sir."

"What is it?"

"She still has deep loyalties to the Viet Minh and with the North. Those ties are well-known here in the South."

"Contact her, Colonel. She has much to offer us," Stone said, considering his options. "I wonder how loyal she is to the commies."

"I will contact her, but it will have to be clandestine. It would not do her much good to be seen negotiating with the American Mission. It would mean trouble for her, especially if Diem gets word."

"Then find an intermediary, someone she approves of but is not a player here in Saigon," the general instructed. "We will remain in the background."

"I think I may know someone. Out of the picture for ten years but the woman knew him well. She often asks about him. I passed the word on to Washington to request they locate him. You never know."

"You got a name?"

"Major Charles Stanek. He was an OSS operative. Donovan spoke very highly of him."

"How do you know him?"

"I met him briefly after the war in '46. We both worked in the Pentagon. He was preparing for his discharge from the army. He's familiar with the country, has quite a story to tell. He met this Madame Thieu and they became close."

"Bring him on board."

"First we must find him, sir."

"Damn it! That's why we have the CIA."

Chapter 2

Charles Stanek had found peace living in the far reaches of Australia, but it did not come without tragedy. He had lost his wife to cancer in 1953. Devastated and left with a four-year old son and a two-thousand-acre sheep and cattle station to run, he had struggled both physically and emotionally to hold things together. With his drovers led by Rusty, his dependable Aborigine foreman, Charlie still managed to build one of the most successful stations in all South Central Australia.

The wall he had carefully built to keep out the world with its troubles and dangers protected him, but he understood all too well that, as a noncitizen in Australia, someone would come knocking one day to take him away. Charlie considered his living situation as a form of self-imposed exile, even though he loved the country and its people.

Having lived in South Australia for only nine years, the country and its people quickly became a part of who he was. The mix of neighbors included, Irish, English, Scots, a spattering of people from the continent and the native Australians. All accepted him into their fold without questions.

Charlie became fascinated with the Aborigines who lived close and all around him. Rusty exposed him and his son George to their culture and religion with its animistic beliefs. Charlie loved its mystery, and intricate balance between the natural and supernatural worlds.

Their culture was alive with spirits—in rocks, bushes, animals. They revered the night sky, with its millions of stars. For Aborigines, the universe—all creation--connected as one cosmic entity. The ideas bewitched him, and he regularly traveled into the bush with Rusty to participate with others of his clan in ceremonies. Soon, after several years, the wind, animals, stars, even the rocks around him spoke to Charlie in much the same way they did to Rusty, but perhaps, with less clarity.

After Jill died, he often lay far out in the bush under the great star-lit sky. These weekly rituals became his way to come to grip with the loss of his wife. The mysteries of the Aborigines' belief system touched his soul deeply,   and he began to believe a strange and inexplicable force beyond his comprehension guided him.

When Charlie spoke to Rusty about his feelings, the Aborigine smiled and nodded. "You are becoming," was how he replied. One day while everyone was in the bush, Rusty approached him from a sacred place. "Boss man," he said, "a spirit will protect you from evil. Always you must remember this."

He believed him.

That was several days before Charlie received his visitors from Canberra.

Rarely a day passed without Charlie wondering when the Cold War world would come crashing in on him. Americans or Russians, it didn't matter. He followed the weeklies and radio news when he could. The Great Powers had negotiated an armistice to end the fighting in Korea, and he read that the French had been defeated in Indochina, leaving the country to victorious Ho Chi Minh's Viet Minh Army. He knew in '45 that it would happen one day. He only hoped the Americans would stay away and allow the Vietnamese to build their own country without outside interference.

He often thought about the people he had met on assignment there in 1945. Khanh, who Charlie called Bob, and especially Madame Thieu, who insisted he call Truin. *Were they still alive? I have not heard.* He had never met a woman quite like Truin—wealthy, politically connected, and dedicated to the cause of independence. Of course, he could not forget that she was also very beautiful. *Will she have a place at the table in a newly independent Vietnam?* He wondered, and smiled at the thought of a woman running the country.

Yet Charlie was very satisfied not to be involved in politics of any kind. He knew the Americans were up to their necks in both Europe and Asia, spending their wealth to stop the spread of communism. *Hell, even the Australians are involved in Cold War politics,* he thought, *doggedly supporting the Americans.*

He tried not to think of Marie spying for the West.

Such a dangerous game Marie plays on the other side of the world. During the war, we met after they dropped me behind German lines with a mission to hook up with partisans and rescue downed pilots. As a teenager with her father, she worked tirelessly with me. We blew up bridges, ambushed German patrols, in addition to rescuing airmen. Then one day late in '44 she left to join forces with Czech General Svoboda in the Carpathians. In October 1944, the Germans defeated them at the Battle of Dukla Pass. Along with thousands of others, the Germans sent Marie to Auschwitz concentration camp. He was overjoyed to learn that the Red Army liberated her near the end of the war.

Forced to return to Central Europe in 1948 when the Russian Intelligence officer, Andre Pavlov, sent me a message stating I must meet him or he will kill Marie and her child. I departed Australia immediately.

For weeks, I played a cat and mouse game with the Soviets before finally escaping with the child. Marie chose to stay as an asset for the CIA buried deep in the Czech government, one of only few agents the Americans had behind the Iron Curtain. Both sides soon knew her as "Rosebud." Only I knew her identity.

Those memories are who I am, and even as a simple sheepherder, I will cherish them always.

Charlie made few trips outside the station, occasionally going into town, but those times were fewer after Jill's death. He knew the CIA tracked his whereabouts, not a difficult task. Even after six years in near isolation, he still knew too much. One day they will come again. Of that, he had little doubt.

The first day of April was a hot, sunny day—they all were. He had sent young George off with Rusty to visit sacred Aborigine places in the hills nearby. With free time on his hands, he prepared to paint the front of their cottage. The last coat was just before the Russians killed the boy's grandfather. *George never knew him,* he thought sadly.

Charlie stepped up the ladder, turned for a second to gaze down the long lane at a lingering plume of dust rising in the still, dry air. *A visitor?* Charlie asked himself. He did not get many and was surprised. Balancing on the wood ladder, he stretched his six feet plus frame to see. Shading his soft blue eyes against the bright sun and dust, he looked into the brown horizon with growing concern.

His blond hair had grown long and straight as baling wire, curling at the base of his neck. Usually, he swept it back under the black Stetson he had purchased several years earlier on his only trip to Sydney.

Charlie did not like visitors of any kind disrupting his work. His jaw tensed, the muscles in his back and shoulders twitched nervously. Visitors often meant trouble and he went out of his way to avoid trouble. He knew his life in Australia depended on that.

His drovers grew to respect his need for solitude. When he first arrived at the station nine years earlier, they challenged him physically, wanting to get his measure. They quickly learned that, due to his superior strength and agility, they were no match.

"Running from the Germans and later the Russians taught me to survive," he told them. "Makes a man tough and a little mean."

For a man barely into his late thirties, he had many stories to tell. Far out into the Outback range with only his drovers around him, he felt comfortable opening up, far away from prying ears. Mostly, he omitted the bad stuff, the secrets countries tortured and killed to possess.

Charlie continued standing on the ladder, suspiciously watching a dark sedan approach. *An ugly car like that...It must be a government agent,* he decided, finally stepping down, taking each step one at a time slowly so he could observe. A frown blistered across his ruggedly handsome, tanned face.

He watched the car park in front of the house. The man on the passenger side slowly rolled his window down. Charlie saw that he was dressed in a suit. That confirmed his suspicions. The two men—not old, not young—conversed with each other, then finally the driver got out and walked to the passenger side. Charlie did not move but continued to watch them.

The passenger got out and both men approached Charlie. He looked both men over, slowly taking their measure. They were younger than he had thought—maybe in their late twenties, trim of build and well groomed. *Look like CIA men to me*, he thought. Both shorter than Charlie by a couple of inches, their skin looked white as Wisconsin snow. *City boys*, he decided. With their hats left in the car, he saw the young men both sported crewcuts. Seeing the haircuts, he knew they had to be government boys.

With skin darkened by a relentless Australian sun, he had allowed his hair to grow, just long enough to protect his head from burning, but short enough so the broad brimmed black Stetson he wore fit comfortably.

Charlie looked hard at them, especially the car's passenger. He figured he could take them if he had to, one at a time, not together at once. They had him if it came to that, and too late to call his drovers over from the bunkhouse. He slowly stepped off the ladder, setting the pail of paint down.

"You lost?" Charlie called to them before they were close to the house. They did not reply, but continued to walk toward him. They stopped only a few feet from where Charlie stood. "You boys hear me? Are you lost?" The two looked at each other, then at Charlie.

"Charles Stanek, Major, United States Army?" the man on the passenger side asked directly, devoid of any curiosity. He seemed to think he found his man.

"Maybe," Charlie replied. "You a tax man?" He tried to smile, but on the sunbaked face it was more of a grimace.

Neither man smiled. "I'm looking for Major Charles Stanek," the man repeated. "Are you he?"

"Name's Stanek, but not in the army. I run this place and I'm damn busy so state your business and get off my land." He stood his ground and did not approach the strangers.

"I got a sealed letter from the American Embassy for Charles Stanek," the passenger said. "It's top priority and time sensitive."

"Ok. You want me to sign for it?" He noticed the man spoke with an American accent while the other had not spoken at all. The speaker had a glum, expressionless face that told Charlie nothing about how he would react if he threw the letter in his face. *Shoot me? I doubt it,* he decided, but knew he would return, and next time, with others supporting him.

"It is for Major Stanek's eyes only." He pulled out a photo, looked at it, then at Charlie.

"I'm ordered to wait while it is read," the American said without emotion but with growing impatience. "Major, please take it and read."

"Yeah? Why'd you bring the Aussie along?" Charlie asked, finally taking the letter. "Just for company or something more?"

The man stepped forward and flashed his credentials. "Immigration Service, Mr. Stanek," he said dryly.

Charlie opened the letter and read. He saw immediately that Jon Grey, Station Agent, signed it. "I've read it so go away. And tell Grey to go to hell. Sorry mates but a wasted trip."

Mr. Stanek, as an illegal alien, I must take you into custody unless you can provide some type of documentation to prove you belong here," the Australian said, also lacking emotion.

"Wait a minute. What kind of trick are you pulling. I'm a tax payer with no criminal record."

Both men shrugged.

"You can come with us peaceful or we can take you to Canberra in chains. Your choice," the Aussie said. "Which is it?"

"It's that important?"

"Very important. I got orders from the Secretary of State directly to bring you to the Embassy," the American stated forcefully.

Hell, it's always important, Charlie thought with growing unease.

"You coming with us?" he demanded to know.

"I have a child, a station to run. Give me the rest of today to put a few things in order, shave, talk to the boys. You can do that, can't you?"

Charlie was marched into the U.S. Embassy the following day by the American who introduced himself as Jack Stover. He gave Charlie barely enough time to say good-bye to George, and give Rusty instructions. Rusty had been through this before seven years ago so he was prepared.

Down a long corridor, he was ushered into a small, out-of-the-way suite of offices and ordered to sit by the same agent.

"What did you say your name is?" he asked.

"Jack Stover," he replied, sitting down near but not beside Charlie.

"You thinking I might run?"

"Not really." Jack Stover smiled. "We'd find you."

Finally, an older, heavier Jon Grey came out of one of two offices. He walked over to Charlie and extended his hand. "Mr. Stanek, please come," he said pointing to the office he had just exited.

"Grey," Charlie, said, standing. "So it is you, isn't it?"

"You remember," Grey said, escorting him. The field agent followed quietly behind. When they entered, Grey said, "Please Stanek, sit down. I have a matter of urgent importance to discuss with you."

The three men sat.

"We meet under much different circumstances," Grey said somberly to begin their meeting. "Such a way with women you have, Stanek." He was looking not at Charlie but seemed to be browsing a single page communique. He finally looked up and smiled.

Charlie recalled what the documents looked like. He had no reply.

"You are certainly one memorable guy," Grey said, appearing to examine Charlie, looking for something—age, physical appearance, or even, trying to probe inside his head. "A real lady's man, aren't you?" He tried to inject a little humor to break the tension.

Still an upper class prick, Charlie thought, remembering him well from their two meetings in Prague. *His sense of moral responsibility compromised simply because he lacked the courage to grab onto what he knew was right and fight for it. Yup, he was a plutocrat born and raised, destined to fuck up the world.* "Couldn't make it in Central Europe, eh Grey?"

Grey ignored the comment. "We have a situation in Southeast Asia you may be able to help us with."

"You dragged me here across Australia, away from my son, to ask for my advice?" Charlie stood with growing anger. "Ever hear of telephones?"

"This is Top Secret, Stanek. A problem that demands much more from us. We need you!"

"You have several problems, I think, Mr. Grey, but none involve me. I have been isolated in the Outback for seven years. I know no one."

"Mr. Stanek, I harbor no hard feelings toward you from our last meeting. Can we move on? Sit down." It sounded like an order.

"I repeat, Mr. Grey. What do you want from me?" Hesitating at first, Charlie finally sat down, knowing leaving would be futile.

"To the point. I like that," Grey said.

"Go on. Give me the situation."

"We, in our efforts to halt the spread of Communism in Asia have supported the current regime in South Vietnam. Bao Dai is President while Ngo Dinh Diem acts as his Prime Minister.

Due to recent events in the country, we have come to realize that Diem is not managing his country well. He seems to have little understanding of the needs of the people and the various sects are rising up against him. In other words, Stanek, Prime Minister Diem has lost the support of the people and must be removed from his office."

"Overthrown, you mean, Grey," Charlie said. "What did you expect? The people support the Viet Minh, the rightful rulers."

"Yes, well. The policy formulated by the present administration includes a stable pro-West regime in Saigon, one capable of meeting existing challenges both internal and foreign."

"The government in Hanoi is considered foreign? Do I have that right?"

"Correct."

"I think we're right back where we were in Prague." Frustrated and angry, Charlie had been dragged from his home to hear this bull, he was direct and demanding. "Regardless, come to the point. What do you want from me?"

Grey smiled. "Yes, to you. We are considering different options to replace Diem but we know little of the various factions exerting power there. The Mission in Saigon has found a contact who is very well informed and promises to be very helpful to us in locating a replacement. This is where you come in, Stanek"

"What you are saying is the Americans don't really understand shit about the internal affairs of Vietnam. With limited ability to speak the language, few advisors who have spent any time there at all, and an almost paranoid fear of the Russians and Chinese, all you really have are theories, an ideology, and statistics. I know the game."

Grey tried his best to ignore the outburst. "Our contact likes Americans and is willing to advise us on a path forward," he continued. "Covertly. It cannot be known in the country that she assists us."

"Good for you. Do it then."

"Not that easy," Grey sighed deeply. Stover had his eyes closed and appeared to be napping.

"Saigon is a hotbed of seditious activities. No one trusts anyone else, and that goes for our contact. She will only work with us, and clandestinely, with you leading our efforts."

"What the hell?"

"The person is your friend from ten years ago. Someone, according to our sources, you were very friendly with, shall we say. Do you remember Madame Thieu? It seems she remembers you well and will only work with you."

Charlie stared at Grey, and then smiled. The smile turned into a laugh. "Well, well, well," he said. "Then you want me to officially represent the United States government?" he asked amused. "Do I have that right?"

Stover's eyes quickly opened. He immediately looked to Grey.

"We want you to negotiate with her on behalf of the U.S. We are requesting that she provide names of political associates who would be more suitable to replace Diem. All very hush hush, of course." Grey continued to stress the secrecy of her involvement. "If Diem discovered her involvement, he would quickly move against them, probably imprison or kill her."

"Tell me more about Madame Thieu. How does she find herself in such a position of power in relation to the U.S.?" Charlie had grown suddenly very curious.

Madame Thieu—Nguyen Phuc Truin—so beautiful and so mysterious. How could I ever forget? She intrigued me from the first time we met in Vung Tau near the ocean. The way she held her head, the light in her eyes, her skin the texture of rare porcelain. Her long black hair tied in a bun held with a hand-carved ivory comb. Yet, as I recall, she stood before me in soldier's fatigues at that first meeting.

I called her Truin. I thought I loved her, but our worlds were so different, She, in a fight for her country's independence, and I an official representative of the U.S. Government. It could never work and we both recognized that.

Charlie sighed, smiled softly, thinking of what could have been.

Looking strangely at Charlie, Grey frowned. "A wealthy and very beautiful woman with deep political ties in the country, including to Bao Dai."

"What about her close relationship with the Viet Minh and the Communists? She is a political operative with an agenda that may not parallel yours," Charlie retorted.

"We've taken that into consideration and are willing to work around it. 'An enemy of my enemy is my friend.' We hope."

"Meaning Diem?" Charlie had his doubts about the whole operation but said nothing.

"We do have leverage, Stanek," Grey said. "She is also a business woman with much to lose if South Vietnam falls to the Communists. Her many investments include a casino, thousands of acres of rice paddy, and a hotel. As you can see, she is in an excellent position to provide us with vital information. A true capitalist after all, eh?"

"Really?" He was obviously impressed with her success, but doubted very much whether she was a capitalist. Charlie considered the information. "How does she know I'm even alive?"

"She had evidently assumed you were still one of our assets. She inquired from our man in Saigon, requesting your whereabouts. He ran that back to Washington, and well, here we are. She believes she can trust you and only you to keep your word."

"So what does that matter? I very much doubt whether you can keep yours," Charlie said.

"I told you this was a bad idea," Stover said. "What's the incentive? He has a life here in Australia." He stood frustrated and left the room to the two men. "Fuck," he whispered to no one as the door shut behind him.

Charlie and Grey silently watched him leave.

"Exactly what do you want from me?" Charlie asked, now intrigued.

"We want you to meet with her and discuss the political situation in South Vietnam. We expect names and information on prominent anti-communist politicians. If you can nail that down your visit will be considered a success." Grey watched Charlie closely while he spoke.

"Will you do that for America?" Grey asked softly. "Of course, you will be given your commission as a major in the United States Army, and will travel as such."

"A short trip to Vietnam to see an old friend? I think I can manage that," Charlie said with interest.

Charlie's abrupt change of attitude did not go unnoticed by Grey.

It would be good to see her again, Charlie thought. *Let me see. She would be in her mid-thirties now. She seems to have done very well, especially in the turbulent world of Vietnam, according to Grey anyway.* Thinking of Truin brought up many memories—good and bad.

"Oh, by the way, you will be accompanied by Stover who will assist as your assistant and advisor. He recently spent a tour there before re-assigned to the station here in Sydney, and he should be very helpful to you."

The bastard is supposed to keep a close eye on me, Charlie knew from experience with the Agency. I know their game. He nodded, knowing they had him in an awkward position. "I want permanent residency here as part of the deal. Can you arrange that?"

"That shouldn't be a problem."
"When do I leave?"
"Tonight, on a supply hop. First to Manila then Saigon."

Chapter 3

The DC-3 hit the runway at Tan Son Nhut airport with a hard bounce. A short and sudden burst of rain caught them as they taxied to the terminal. Charlie looked out the window through the steam and shimmers of heat rising from the concrete. *Not too much has seemed to change,* he thought, seeing mostly military vehicles around the same large yellow stucco building surrounded by palm trees. The sandbagged machine gun positions now replaced by concrete bunkers, and several jet planes lined up near the field. *I didn't know exactly who controlled the airfield in '45, and I don't really know who does today.* He smiled at that, although it made him feel a little nervous.

Those days, he remembered, had been both exhilarating and dangerous:

September 1945 and the streets of Saigon were aflame with insurrection. Vietnamese rose up after the British released French soldiers from Japanese confinement. The Vietnamese, demanding independence from their French colonizers, immediately attacked the freed soldiers.

The war with Japan was over and they were surrendering all their bases in Indochina. Neither the British nor American were prepared to occupy the entire French colony, so the British decided to release French soldiers to assist, not trusting native Indochinese. The soldiers immediately began to reassert French rule, much to the Vietnamese leader's chagrin.

The British assigned by the Allied Control Commission to take the Japanese surrender in Saigon while Chiang Kai chek's Nationalist Chinese forces accepted it in Hanoi. The Chinese were much more deferential to Vietnamese self-rule, but the British welcomed the French back to "preserve order."

I arrived in Saigon in September after the street riots of days earlier to investigate the violent death of an Americans OSS agent working with the British. I saw first-hand that the age of colonialism was rapidly drawing to a close. Everywhere in the French colony, the people demanded independence. Organized resistance to their renewed rule began immediately under the leadership of Ho Chi Minh's Viet Minh.

The short hop from Manila was uneventful. Charlie had taken the time to get to know Stover better. *We're going to be together for the next week, so I had better get to know who this guy is,* he decided. He learned that Jack was 28, educated at NYU, and single—no attachments. The agency recruited him right out of college. *Typical,* Charlie thought, knowing the intelligence services like to get their people young. *He probably had not been around long and lacked tough espionage experience--green,* he decided upon a quick assessment. *But Grey did say he spent a tour in Vietnam.*

"Jack, what did you do here? Train, advise, or spy?"

"Nothing like that," he replied. "Jon was trying to embellish my record so you would feel like I had enough experience here to be helpful."

"He lied," Charlie said flatly.

"One might say that."

"What's your mission and expertise?"

"I'm assigned to Grey. His aid, I guess," Jack said. "But I'm a trained linguist. I speak fluent Chinese. My parents were missionaries in China before the Commies took over. I was born there."

"That language won't help you much here," Charlie said.

"You'd be surprised."

Nothing about the CIA would surprise me, Charlie thought. *But I've learned the hard way; they have a purpose, always a purpose in anything they do. So, my assistant speaks fluent Chinese and here we are in Indochina. Interesting.*

They marched through the terminal without problems. They flashed their passports and quickly were out hailing a cab. Charlie noticed immediately that Jack was content to follow his lead dealing with customs.

Jack dabbed at his face with a handkerchief. "Whew, this place is worse than Central Australia," he said.

"Humidity, Jack. Better get used to it," Charlie replied. "You'll need to ditch your suit for something lighter." Charlie wore a simple cotton shirt and slacks, prepared for the climate. "Something that doesn't say "CIA" on it." He smiled.

"Yeah, see what you mean," Jack said, peeling off the jacket to expose his weapon in the small of his back.

Charlie saw it and smiled. "Don't worry none about the pistol. I think half the country is probably armed." He saw a dark French sedan approach them slowly.

"I think we got a taxi," Charlie announced.

The older Citroen pulled up beside them. An older man jumped out and ran to the curb. Both men watched.

"Okay Major, We go now," the man said, beaming. He grabbed their satchels and opened the door. "In, we go."

Charlie paused, surprised. "What? Who the hell are you?"

The man looked disappointed. "You no remember me? Your good buddy, Khanh. I hurt."

Charlie stopped and stared at the smaller man. "Bob? I remember. How could I forget my good friend, Bob."

They embraced.

"Long time, I think. 1948 in Singapore," Bob said, looking Charlie over carefully. He shook his head. "You tough man, Major. Beat Russians." He laughed then got in the Citroen. "Same car. You remember near Pleiku?"

"I will never forget," Charlie said.

Jack listened to the conversation, surprised. "Grey is right. You seem to be a hard man to forget, Stanek."

"What a coincidence," Charlie said, but believing there is no such thing.

"No, I know you come here. We know..."

Charlie was perplexed, "How?"

"Madame tell me," Bob said. "She know about everything in Saigon." He motioned to his ears. "She have many spies— Vietnamese, French, American. No matter."

They flew down the narrow streets.

"Does he know where we're going?" Jack asked.

"Bob, where are you taking us? To the Hotel Continental? The Majestic?" Charlie asked.

"No, no, no. I take you to Dragon House. You like."

"Dragon House," Charlie repeated.

"Madame's hotel. Very nice, quiet, peaceful. You talk, eh?"

"You heard the man, Jack. Any problems with that?"

Jack shrugged. "Fine with me."

Bob smiled. "You like, Major's friend. You treated top-notch."

Bob rifled through the narrow congested streets like a bullet. Street vendors with their carts, pedestrians, even animals scattered to make way for the Citroen. Driving with one hand on the wheel, Bob motioned with other, pointing out landmarks. The two Americans held on for dear life.

They pulled into the drive of a small boutique hotel, brightly painted with well- manicured lawns surrounding. Charlie noticed the opera house sitting as regally as he remembered it behind the Dragon House on Rue de la Liberte. Down the street, he saw the Intercontinental and Majestic dominating the skyline.

A young man ran to greet them as Bob jumped out to open the doors for his guests. He took their few pieces of luggage and ushered them into the hotel. Inside, elegance equal to any in Europe or the States greeted them. Charlie was impressed and he was certain Jack was, too.

At the desk, a very attractive young woman greeted them. Bob spoke briefly and the woman nodded and smiled. "Welcome to Vietnam," she said.

Charlie and Jack signed the register while she watched. "You are our guests here so please...Madame waits your arrival."

"Good, I look forward to seeing her again," Charlie replied. "It's been a long time."

Jack smiled and nodded, taking his cues from Charlie.

"Charlie and Jack. I will remember," she said. She looked to an older man and he approached from somewhere in the lobby.

"First class all the way. Nothing but the best for you, Major. I'm glad I got this gig."

"I'm really happy you're so content, but keep your eyes open, Jack," Charlie cautioned him.

The older man took their pieces of luggage and pointed for them to follow. In the elevator and up three floors, he led them first to Charlie's room and then to Jack's. Charlie looked around the room, impressed. *Luxury accommodations*, he thought, *fit for a prince or princess*. But Charlie wasn't stupid. He quickly searched the room for listening devices. He knew it was too early to trust his hostess.

Before he could test the softness of the bed, there was a soft knock at the door. He opened it, expecting Jack. He was pleasantly surprised to see Truin standing there. She wore a white silk Ao Dai with red dragons printed on it.

At first, they just stared. *She's as beautiful as I remember*, Charlie thought. *Fuller in the figure but still trim in a manner he could only describe as elegant.* "Truin," Charlie said softly. "You are as I remember, maybe more beautiful." He stood not knowing what else to do. Finally, "Come in, please."

"Charlie," she replied, entering the room. "I would have known you anywhere." Wanting urgently to touch him, she wasted no time. She reached out to hold his hands. "Not a day passed that I did not think of you."

Without another word spoken, they embraced, not as friends or representatives of alien cultures, but as lovers. For both, the many years that had passed did nothing to diminish their passion for each other. Charlie wrapped his arms around her slim body to pull her closer. They kissed.

Charlie immediately noticed the difference in Truin that came with ten years. This woman was mature, seemed more complete, and radiated a confidence that comes with age and hard experience. He saw it in the deep brown eyes. They were hard yet knowing, and reminded him of his mother's, yet Truin could not be more than 32-35 years of age.

Yes, Charlie had seen those eyes before. *In Central Europe...from another war. Those ten years had made Truin a woman, a woman who took what she wanted, and once she had it, would die before she gave it up*, he thought, remembering Marie.

"We have much to talk about, Charlie," she whispered. "I must know everything about you these last ten years. The Russians. I heard they had captured you, and wanted to send you to their cold north lost forever. Yet, here you are." She touched his face softly.

"How...?"

"Ong Giau told me this. He learned it from a Russian soldier." She smiled. "The world is not so large, Charlie."

He nodded and they again embraced. Hearing a noise from the open doorway, they looked up from each other. "Jack," Charlie said. "Let me introduce Truin, Madame Thieu, our hostess. Truin, Jack Stover." She bowed while Jack prepared to shake hands, but nodded instead.

"Major, I must remind you. We are to meet with General Stone in an hour."

"Yes," Charlie replied. "Truin, later we must talk, so much to talk about."

"Charlie, tonight, then you will tell me of your child. I must hear all about him." She smiled mysteriously.

That surprised him. *How did she know of my son? Spies are everywhere*, he decided, but he was particularly concerned that knowledge of his son circulated around the world. "We will talk, Truin," he said and turned to Jack.

Charlie and Jack met with General Stone at the headquarters of the Saigon Military Assistance Group. The Building was a small shabby building in downtown Saigon near the Intercontinental Hotel. The American military advisors were few in number. Stone told Charlie that only 350 men were trying to cover most of Indochina.

"What kind of assistance do you provide, General? Charlie asked curious.

"Small arms and training mostly. We have been distributing them to anti-communist groups opposing the Viet Minh."

"What about the army here in the south? Are the generals competent and loyal to Diem?" Jack asked.

"Stone shrugged. "Competent? I have my doubts. All units commanded by Vietnamese officers will be turned over to the government of South Vietnam by July 1. The French announced that earlier this year."

"Diem then will have control over all of the military?"

"Yes."

"So it may be much more difficult to replace him when that occurs," Jack said. "It must be done quickly."

"As soon as we can find a suitable replacement."

"By suitable you mean what?" Charlie asked.

"Someone capable of running a democratic government, of course, and is anti-communist and pro-American."

"Stressing the latter two, eh General?"

Stone smiled. "Yes."

"Would a left wing politician be acceptable to Washington?"

"Someone we can work with."

That's vague, Charlie thought. "What about the scheduled elections next year?"

"Per the Geneva agreements? "We'll see what develops, eh?"

"I think Madame Thieu will insist on free elections in 1956 regardless of who is in charge here."

"Secretary Dulles likes Diem but we very much doubt whether he can effectively rule the country, and I think the Secretary is having strong reservations about continuing with the present regime. We must act now to replace him before things change," the general went on. "Just now the National Front composed of several religious sects and the criminal element has seized a couple of provinces. Events are pressing in on Diem, I think."

"What do you want from me?" Charlie asked. "From Madame Thieu?"

"We must find a politician here willing to replace Diem. Someone who can rule the country and is ant-communist, of course."

"And pro-American."

"Remember for the U.S., the primary objective to halting the spread of communism. If one country in Southeast Asia falls, they will all be overrun. I'm certain of it. You know... like dominoes."

"What can you offer her for her assistance?"

The general thought for a moment. "We will ensure elections will be held next year; the French Army will be gone from all of Indochina immediately; and if she so desires, we will find her a place in the new government." He looked hard at Charlie. "We need to know her contacts here in the south. The North is leaving Viet Minh cadre behind. Find out who they are," he said, still watching him.

Charlie listened quietly and nodded when the general was finished. *Not much to offer her,* he decided. *Hell, nothing really. She's probably not interested in a role in the government; she expects elections to be held; and the French are whipped anyway. Hmm.*

"I will be speaking with her over the next week. I will pass on the American offer, and we'll see what happens," he said, preparing to stand.

"I've read that you have done outstanding work for us here in Vietnam and in Europe. Major. I'm certain you'll find a way to get what we need."

"I'll be in contact," Charlie said, standing.

"Excellent. We'll meet in several days to see what you have come up with," Stone said. "Good day, gentlemen."

Charlie waited for the general to leave, and then turned to follow him from the small box of a room.

"Not a chance in hell, she will go along with the program, Jack," Charlie said on the walk back to the Dragon House. "It's almost insulting. I don't think the general is leveling with me." He continued to voice his suspicions. "Much more is going on I don't know about."

"Hey, do you really care? You just go back to Australia to your ranch or whatever it is, and continue with your life. Things here will sort themselves out."

Charlie did not reply. *I have more at stake here than gathering information,* he thought with growing concern. "I think they've placed me right in the middle of some type of potential power struggle."

"Vietnam is not your concern, Jack replied.

Charlie said nothing.

"The middle?" Jack stopped and turned to Charlie. "You are a special envoy of the United States Government, so follow orders and get on with it. Remember that."

"The woman is my friend and I can't sacrifice her for American policy. Keep that in mind. Ten years ago, she saved my life. I owe her."

Jack, not really understanding, just nodded.

The general's statement about locating Viet Minh cadre still stuck in his mind. *Am I an envoy or a spy?* he asked himself sullenly as they entered the grand lobby of the Dragon House.

Chapter 4

Charlie lay awake under the silk sheets trying to sleep while the ceiling fan whirred above him. He was troubled. His meeting with the American general still disturbed him, and he tried to reason through it. He needed to come up with a plan, but his thoughts continued to return to Truin. Seeing her again rekindled feelings, he thought he would never have again after Jill's death.

He reconsidered his role, but he knew he was only a means to an end. *To them we are nothing more than expendable pieces on a chessboard, played then discarded when no longer needed. How can I protect her?* he asked himself. How can I protect her and accomplish my mission satisfactorily.

He gave up trying to sleep. *I need a walk, a long walk around downtown Saigon,* he decided. He dressed and prepared to leave. Since dinner at the hotel with Jack, he had been in his room. Truin was nowhere around and that was good because he needed more time to think. He walked through the large lobby and felt many eyes on him. The young woman he had met behind the front desk was gone and in her place was an older man. He seemed to take no interest in Charlie's departure, but others casually lounging or working watched indiscreetly. *I'm an oddity, I guess.*

He stepped out into the night air, immediately struck by a dense bank of wet still air that almost took his breath away. The many fans in the hotel kept the air moving, and made things slightly more tolerable than the polluted air along the street. He walked along the wide boulevard toward the Intercontinental.

The Hotel Intercontinental suffered serious damage in September 1945 from the fighting between the Vietnamese and French. How dingy and gray everything seemed then. Entering the lobby, its grandeur awed him with ornate decoration and furnishings. People—Vietnamese, French, even a few Americans and Europeans mingled with drinks and conversation. *Just where I want to be*, he thought smiling. Struggling around bodies, he made his way to the bar where a young Vietnamese bartender greeted him. He immediately began speaking in French.

"American," Charlie said.

The man nodded, "Oh, American?"

"Shot of American Bourbon, straight up. You got it?"

"We have." He turned to grab a bottle from the shelf, a bottle of "Four Roses." "You like?"

"Double," Charlie ordered.

The young man quickly poured him the drink, and stood back to watch him take a swallow.

"Bottoms up," Charlie said, held the glass up then threw it down. "Another please."

Impressed, the young bartender poured him another, nodded, and went on with his business, his curiosity apparently satisfied. Charlie turned to look over the crowd. Mostly men, he saw. Several had Vietnamese women hanging on their arms. He noticed a younger Caucasian woman in a far corner alone, tall and attractive, she stood out above the others. Charlie with his drink casually walked over to where she stood.

"Charlie Stanek from Australia, here alone and want some conversation," he said. "Can you help me?"

The woman smiled. "Depends," she said.

"On what?"

"On what you want us to talk about."

From her accent, he knew she was American. Thin with deep brown hair and blue eyes, he thought her attractive in a wholesome, Wisconsin kind of way. "How about Wisconsin?"

"I don't know anything about Wisconsin. How about California?" she said smiling.

"You didn't tell me your name," Charlie said.

"Betty. Betty McCarthy, born and raised Californian," she said. "You been to the great state of California?"

"Don't know much about the place, so I guess I'll have to make things up."

"I'll probably know when you are, Mr. Stanek."

Charlie paused. "I remember the beaches, Very beautiful, much like Australia's. Why did you leave them?"

"My job takes me all over the world, even to places like this," she said looking around her. "I work for the *Los Angeles Times*. Reporter. What do you do, Mr. Stanek?"

"I'm a rancher in central Australia. Sheep mostly, on a couple thousand acres."

"I don't know much about that place, but I bet it's beautiful."

"What kind of story brings you here, Betty?" he asked. "Kind of remote. Isn't Europe where all the action is? You know...Cold War and all."

She shrugged and took a drink. "Old news, Charlie. I think there's more action here."

"Really? What kind of action?"

"A new hot spot, with the French leaving and the Americans taking their place. Maybe the next war to halt the commies, since Korea has cooled down," Betty said, sounding like she knew what she was looking for, but mostly to Charlie, it seemed like she had a firm grasp of the situation in Asia. "I'm mostly interested in the political and social dynamics here. You know… the human interest stuff. My readers want to read about the men and women here, who they are, and what they want."

"Whew, I'm impressed that you have such a handle on what you're writing."

"Yeah, it's competitive," she said, appearing to feel she said enough. "Why are you here? And by the way, why do you have an American accent?"

"Does everyone need a reason for coming to Saigon?" He tried to avoid answering the latter question.

"Pretty much," Betty replied. "You selling the Vietnamese wool? Probably not. Lamb chops?" She gave him a smile that swallowed him.

"Nothing like that," Charlie replied, finishing his drink. "Just visiting an old friend."

"You picked a dangerous place to be a tourist. Must be a close friend."

"We were close."

"Ok, I gotcha," she replied. "So why Wisconsin?"

Charlie felt her eyes looking him over, sizing him up. "I was born and raised there. After the war I decided I needed a change of scenery so I moved south," he said finally and reluctantly answering the question.

"You sure did." She moved closer to him, her breast under the loose silk touching his shoulder. "Now South Vietnam. That's really getting away from the Midwest."

"A short visit."

"Is your friend here?" She looked around the crowd. "Australian, American, male or female?"

"Vietnamese. Someone I met during the war…with the Japanese."

"Not by chance Prime Minister Diem, is it? He an old buddy of yours?" she said. "If he is, please introduce me. I'd love an interview."

"Don't know him. My friend runs a hotel a couple of blocks from here—the Dragon House."

"Madame Thieu is your friend, eh?"

"You know her?"

"No, but I understand she is very well-known in the city."

Charlie was surprised. "Really?"

"The Viet Minh heiress, she is called. I hear the Americans have become very interested in her."

"Why's that?"

"She is very well-connected. Even Prime Minister Diem wants to know what she knows, especially after the shoot-out he had with the local gangster, a person by the name of Bay Vien, who is a partner of your friend. They own a large casino here in Saigon—very elegant and very profitable. It's called Le Grand Monde. I suggest you have a look, Charlie."

"You are very well-informed. How long you been here?"

"In and out since the battle up north that basically ended the Vietnamese war with the French."

"I'll look forward to seeing the casino then." He looked around, checked his watch, and then returned to his conversation with Betty."

"Leaving?" She got the hint. "Here, Charlie Stanek is my card. If you can help a poor underpaid journalist, let me know. I'm staying here, where I might add, most foreigners stay."

"Thanks." Charlie took the card and put it in his shirt pocket. "I probably won't be here long enough to be of service to you, Betty, but good luck with your story."

"I'm here most every night," she said with a smile.

Charlie left the Intercontinental to walk back in the direction of Dragon House. *Shit, an American journalist,* he thought. *That's all I need.* Before he reached the street, he heard his name called.

"Major, Major, here," he heard, then a man jumped from his vehicle and ran toward him.

"Bob," Charlie said surprised. "Working, eh?"

"Every night," Bob replied. "Where you go?"

He considered the question. "Since I have a ride now, how about Madame Thieu's casino. I've heard so much about it."

"I take you, yes?"

"Let's go." Bob ushered him into the back of the Citroen and he got in front. Before casino, how about I show you city. Long time since last visit."

"I would like that."

Bob roared off. He began his tour by pointing out different buildings—hotels, government offices, shops, and evening attractions. As they moved out from the center of the city, he, without explaining, showed Charlie Saigon's more strategic assets. "Where National Army is, over here the American Mission, there the old French prison. You remember from before?"

"I remember," Charlie replied, recalling the Japanese police officer, Major Hiroaka, who operated the Saigon jail during the war. *A very determined and honorable man*, Charlie thought. He tried to take everything in. He was surprised that so little had actually changed since '45. He felt comfortable giving Bob his impressions.

"The war, but soon we rebuild," Bob replied.

"Peace has come?"

"Maybe, but many problems."

"Will the Bao Dai government provide peace?"

Bob shrugged. "Vietnam no want a king. We want elections like in U.S., eh? Next year, we have elections and whole country together—one country. U.S., France promise."

Hopeful, Charlie thought, feeling sad that everything will probably depend on the great powers. "How is your family?"

"My wife good, strong woman. Two sons grow up."

"They live in Saigon with you?"

"No," Bob replied with sadness in his voice. "They away. Oldest in Jungle. Still fighting there. I worry."

"Sons in the National Army?"

"No," he said abruptly. "Tomorrow or next day, I show you Vietnam outside Saigon, but very dangerous. We go with Madame Thieu," he said to change the subject.

Trucks filled with soldiers passed them, barreling down the street.

"Where do you think they're going?" Charlie asked curious.

"I think they search for a general who can lead them."

Both laughed.

"No peace for Vietnam yet," Bob said finally. "Many people no like Prime Minister Diem. They say his government not have mandate to rule Vietnam."

"What about Madame Thieu? What does she believe?"

Bob, at first, was hesitant to reply. "She is caught in middle. Now very afraid," he said cautiously.

"Afraid? For her life?"

"French soldiers kill her husband and son. They say Viet Minh and must die. Now her? She too powerful among the people. President Diem watch her."

"People like you, Bob?"

"Yes. Two month ago, she gave her land to the farmers. Ask no money. Rich who own most land now hate her for that. Madame Thieu say government land reform no good. They only stop rent increases, no more. She say we must do more. 'The farmers should own their land,' she declare in newspaper. The rich hate her for that. So many enemies. I worry."

"Things have to get better," Charlie said, trying to put a positive spin on the situation.

The hour was late when they pulled up in front of the casino. Charlie got out and offered to pay.

"No, no please," Bob said. "I wait for you."

Charlie nodded.

He was shocked to see such a lively, decadent place in a small war-torn country. Packed with Vietnamese and foreigners, it vibrated with activity. The hum of roulette wheels and crowd noise was everywhere. A blue cloud of tobacco smoke hung above the action. Struck by the sound of laughter and shouts of joy, he decided the leisure class had traded tomorrow with all its problems for an evening of mindless merriment. *The five percent who own Vietnam*, he decided, looking around at the white and brown faces. *The fat cats, my father, a big union man would say.*

In the casino, the many soldiers in their uniforms interested him, and they represented different countries—France, South Vietnam, and even the United States. Like over-stuffed peacocks, perspiration covering their faces, they laughed and drank. He saw the American general standing at a roulette wheel, head and shoulders above the others.

Not exactly blending into the group around him, Charlie thought, walking over to stand behind him. "Winning the hearts of the people, General?" he asked flatly.

The general turned to see who was behind him. "Major Stanek," he said but very distracted. "Going to have a go at it?" He continued to watch the spinning wheel.

"Just catching the action, sir." He noticed the well-dressed man standing beside the general. Charlie nodded stiffly to him.

"Let me introduce you, Major. Mr. Bay Vien, owner of this establishment. Major Stanek is a special envoy sent by Washington," the general said and quickly returned to his game.

"Have you come to make peace, sir?" the older Vietnamese asked, with a hint of sarcasm.

"I'm just learning my way around," Charlie replied, understanding it was an idle, meaningless question.

"Have you spoken with our Prime Minister yet?"

Suddenly the wheel stopped. "I win!" the general exclaimed and everyone took notice.

Vien patted the general on the back. "You see," he said to Charlie in perfect English. "Everyone wins here, even the Americans."

"Is that important?"

"Oh yes," he replied quickly. "It seems now we must please you Americans."

Charlie forced a smile but his face said nothing. "I'm learning that in Vietnam that's very important."

Vien gave Charlie a hard look, then suddenly laughed. "Yes, very." He stepped in front of Charlie to talk again with the general.

"Gentlemen, I will leave you to your game," Charlie said to their backs. He turned and walked away. As he walked through the crowd, he remembered what Bob had told him about the recent land reform enacted in South Vietnam. He wondered if anyone here cared about rice paddies. *Do they really need that rent? Probably not,* he decided.

After a couple of drinks, Charlie decided he had seen enough. He walked out into the night air where Bob greeted him. "To the Dragon House," he directed. A steady stream of gamblers came and went from the casino. Most by taxi, he noticed.

Bob nodded and opened the door for him. "Have you ever gambled here, Bob?" he asked inside the Citroen.

Bob turned to Charlie but said nothing, looking at the American as if he were joking. He pulled into the street. "I must feed my family," he finally replied.

Charlie saw that Bob had little respect for those inside the casino. *Born with the wrong pedigree*, he thought, but he knew in his heart that history was probably on Bob's side. He remembered the young revolutionaries gathered in the streets of Prague following the collapse of the Benes government.

Charlie thought he knew which side the Americans would ultimately choose. *Lacking a past with its long traditions, we tend to treat other, older cultures with contempt. To think that we can rebuild Vietnam in our image is the height of folly,* he long believed. He had learned much from Rusty and the Aborigines of Australia during his ten years working with them. As ancient as any culture on the planet, yet Australians were intent on destroying it, something he discovered while living there.

Chapter 5

Charlie lay awake in the early morning darkness, fans whirred, but the heat and humidity still disrupted his sleep. His thoughts ran through the last 24 hours. *With the competing factions struggling for power and the Americans added to the mixture, we have a very volatile situation,* he was quickly learning. *I'll focus on Truin and gathering whatever information I can from her, give it to the general, then get the hell out of here,* he decided. *That's the plan.*

He heard a soft knock on the door. He looked at his watch—6:00 AM. He rolled out of bed, grabbed his trousers and slowly dragged himself to the door. "Yeah?" he asked through the door.

"Major Stanek? I have message for you," a female voice said. "Please?"

Charlie opened the door to the young woman he met the day before behind the desk. "She bowed and smiled. "I sorry, but from Madame." The young woman looked Charlie over as quickly as polite manners would allow while handing him the message. "Sorry," she repeated.

"What's your name?" Charlie asked, reaching for the folded slip of paper.

"Co Vouc," she replied, eyes lowered. "I desk clerk."

"I remember."

"Madame my aunt."

"Of course she is," he said with a smile. "Thank you."

She turned and hurriedly departed for the elevator.

Charlie read the note from Truin. "Charlie, we go to Delta at 7:00. Come alone." *Well, that explains the early morning visit,* he thought. *What do I tell Jack?*

An hour later, Charlie stood at the front desk waiting for Truin. He handed Co Vouc a note addressed to Jack Stover. *Have a private meeting with Madame Thieu. Take the day off,* the note read. A few minutes later, Truin joined him and they departed. Bob waited in the Citroen.

Saigon's narrow, congested streets filled with autos, but mostly with pedestrian traffic. Vendors were setting up their stalls, children ran in and out of the traffic, with armed men mixing with the crowds. It took the three more than an hour to escape the city, but once on the road, Bob accelerated the old Citroen.

"Where exactly are we going?" Charlie finally asked, sitting alone in the back seat. All the windows rolled down as the temperature quickly rose under the bright sunshine.

Truin turned and smiled. "Charlie, we go south to My Tho in the Delta. We visit Khanh's son."

Charlie nodded, but did not understand why. He knew Bob's son was in the area but why did he need to meet them. He was confused.

Truin sensed his confusion. "He was a soldier but now must hide from National Army. I think it important you see for yourself."

"Ok," Charlie replied. Bob slowed as they came upon a roadblock.

"Your passport, Charlie."

He handed it to her as they stopped. "Soldiers?" Charlie asked.

"No, they belong to Binh Xuyen," Truin replied.

The two-armed men took their IDs, looked casually at them, and then handed them back. Without further conversation, they waved the car through.

"Vien's men are everywhere here, Charlie. Diem's soldiers are around Saigon. They afraid to come here. Confusing, yes?"

"It's like the American Old West. Whoever has the most guns is in charge," he replied. "How far to My Tho?"

"Not far, but we go to small fishing hamlet close."

Bob stopped the Citroen, parking it beside a smaller concrete house with a thatched roof and open windows without glass. Children came from everywhere and nowhere to swarm the car. Bob quickly got out with a burlap bag and began handing out chocolate bars. The children excitedly grabbed at the candy. *All about my son's age*, Charlie thought, watching with Truin. Bob spoke to them when the bag was empty and the children stepped back and quickly dispersed. He then reached in the car window and honked the horn three times.

Charlie saw the action. *Must be some type of signal,* he thought.

Suddenly, from behind the house, a young man appeared, a rifle slung across his shoulder. He was dressed in khaki and black with a conical shaped straw hat. He beamed broadly at Bob, bowed, and the two embraced.

"Khanh's son," Truin replied smiling at the reunion. He greeted Truin and soon the three were speaking quietly among themselves. Charlie had no idea the subject of the conversation.

Finally, Bob turned to Charlie. "My son. Quac."

Charlie shook the young man's hand.

"American friend," Bob said proudly to his son. "He asks if you French. I tell him you sent by President of United States."

Charlie said nothing.

"Come," Truin said. She took Charlie's arm. "I take you to village chief. We talk."

While they walked across the dirt road, more and more armed men appeared. They kept their distance, seemingly content to watch the visitors from the shadows of the houses. Charlie noticed and resisted going further.

Turin saw his hesitancy. "No worry. They protect village."

"From who?" Charlie asked.

Truin gave him a strange look. "From the National Army, Charlie." Seeing he still did not understand, she continued. "They fight French. Now they wait."

"For what?"

"They wait to see who will rule Vietnam. They wait for elections next year."

Charlie followed her into a larger well-kept house where an elderly man and his wife waited. They stood to greet them, then offered chairs and hot tea all the while talking among themselves. Still Charlie understood not a word.

Finished, Truin turned to him. "He very angry and worried about his people. Government betraying Vietnamese people, he say. He want to know who Americans support—Ho Chi Minh or Bao Dai."

Charlie had no answer, but he knew he had to say something. Before he could speak, they heard noises from outside. Truin went to the door and looked out. "Men from the National Front, Vien's soldiers," she announced.

Armed men jumped from the rear of a single truck. They began to round up villagers, yelling and pushing them.

"What?" Charlie asked, getting up, also.

"They want money. For taxes to protect village, they say."
Everyone left the house except Bob's son.

Truin began to speak with the man she believed in charge.
Charlie heard her introduce herself. The man bowed then called
to his men. They released the villagers and began to return to
the truck. Their leader looked hard at Charlie but said nothing.

Soon they departed. *Probably up the road to the next
village,* Charlie thought.

"You see, Charlie. No one in charge here in south, so
everyone, even common criminals, think they can do what
they want."

Returning to Saigon, they easily passed through Vien's
roadblock, but nearing the city, they came across another, this
one manned by uniformed men. "National Army," Truin said,
appearing surprised by the roadblock. They again handed
their IDs to the armed men, but this roadblock was not as easy
to escape.

"They tell us to get out," Bob said. When the three were out
and standing on the road surrounded by the soldiers, two men
searched the car.

The officer in charge, a lieutenant Charlie decided, ordered
that one of his men bring Truin to him. He held her ID in his
hand, staring at it. Charlie watched as the soldier, a short,
heavyset man with a thin mustache, dressed impeccably in
his uniform. He began to speak to her and she replied in short
declarative sentences. Their voices rose, and finally the officer
called to two men. They took Truin by the arms and escorted
her to the Jeep.

The soldiers had ignored Charlie and Bob. A young soldier
returned their IDs and motioned for them to go. "What's going
on?" Charlie asked.

"They take her to their headquarters in Saigon." Bob was disturbed but he quickly understood there was nothing he could do.

"No," Charlie said defiantly. "Follow me." He approached the young officer as he was preparing to leave in the Jeep. "I'll speak, you translate," he said to Bob.

"Let her go," Charlie directed and Bob translated. "I am a special envoy from the President of the United States, and this woman is under my orders and protection."

The officer stared at him while Bob translated.

"So what?" he replied with contempt.

"If you do not release her immediately, I will file a formal protest with Prime Minister Diem." He pulled out a pen and small notebook. "What is your name?" he asked. "Your unit?"

He prepared to write it down.

"How do I know who you are?" the Lieutenant replied. He appeared confused.

"Look again at my passport and papers." He retrieved a letter given him by General Stone that appointed him. "I am Major Charles Stanek, United States Army. I am on a special mission to Vietnam. This document states that I am who I say I am, with the authorization to appoint Madame Thieu as my aide and interpreter." Bob translated. Charlie pointed to the letter, but it gave no mention of the authorization, merely recognizing Charlie.

The lieutenant at first seemed confused. "Why her?" he asked. "I have orders to bring her in."

"She is assisting me by permission of the American general and Prime Minister Diem. I must insist you release her." Bob translated. Charlie quickly folded the letter and stuck it in his pocket with his passport.

Silence reigned around the Jeep as the lieutenant pondered his next move. His men watched, smoking and talking quietly among themselves.

The lieutenant nodded to his men in the Jeep. He spoke but several words and they released Truin.

"Let's get out of here," Charlie said, holding Truin's arm. "Bob?"

"Yes, sir, Major," he said relieved.

"Thank you, Charlie," Truin said as they pulled away.

That evening, Charlie stood in the shower as the cold water trickled over him, feeling he had to clear his head. *Just like in '45,* he thought, dismayed. *Everyone has his own agenda. Events swirl around me, and...*He heard a noise.

The curtain pulled back. Truin stood before him. She was naked.

"You are a great man, Charlie." She admired him slowly then stepped in beside him. "I knew it must be you if I talk to the Americans."

They embraced passionately, as if no time had passed between them.

Later, in the darkness of his room alone again, Charlie knew what he had to do. *I got a kid. I can't stay here to sort out the mess. But I can't just abandon her.* He got out of bed to stand on the balcony. He looked out over the city, and thought about his son, hoping that Rusty and the boys were taking good care of him. *Damn it. My first responsibility is to him now.* He felt torn, pulled between them.

Fatherhood was new to Charlie, but he was determined to raise him properly, much like his parents raised him. *Milwaukee.* He smiled, remembering his hometown. Yet, the idea that they would tap Truin for information and then discard her was unacceptable.

Chapter 6

Several days passed, and then a week, still Charlie and Truin avoided the negotiations the general had urgently requested. They spent most days catching up on each other's life. She told Charlie about the Vietnamese war against the French and the loss of her husband, Pham Troung Dinh, and their son. He remembered Dinh, that meeting with him in Vung Tau. *An angry and demanding young man who he had a bad feeling about,* he thought at the time. Charlie instantly did not like him.

Charlie told her about his journey to Central Europe to rescue Marie and the child. He described his meeting with General Pavlov. Truin had met the general in Hanoi in 1946. "Yes, he was a monster," she admitted.

Seldom did they leave Charlie's room. Co Vouc brought them meals early in the morning when it was cool. They made love in the morning, afternoon, and evening. They lay together for hours, talking. He held her close, touching her, feeling her strength pressed against him. Their lives—the ten years between them—had been so different, yet similar. Both in their own personal struggles, they had been caught up in powerful forces beyond their control. Wars, revolution, great power politics had shaped their lives.

He touched her breast, feeling the warmth of her skin as she slept curled in his arms. She moaned softly and kissed his cheek. *So vulnerable,* he thought, *yet a strong woman who has survived so much.* He bent to kiss her then smiled content. Yes, Charlie was in love again.

Jack grew impatient, visiting Charlie's room each afternoon for an update on their talks. "The general wants to know what progress you've made," he told Charlie each day, and each day, he replied, "She's briefing me on the situation and giving me her perspective. The politics here are crazy. It's anarchy. I have to sort it out," he said, but knowing it was more than just buying time.

Jack would stare, growl, and stomp away. *What else could he do,* Charlie knew. After the last several weeks with the agent, he saw that Jack was the nervous, follow-orders-to-the-T kind of person, and very indoctrinated. *He is not too flexible and I must work with that,* Charlie decided, after having thrown him out for the third time.

After each visit, Charlie told him "tomorrow," and finally one day, Jack refused to leave, insisting on something to give the general. Truin left to conduct business in her hotel so the two men were alone.

"Sit down, Jack," he said. "I'll give you what I've learned."

Jack sat and pulled out a pad prepared to write.

"She insists on a full guarantee from the U.S. Government that fair, countrywide elections will be held next year per the agreements at Geneva. Can we do that, Jack?

He shrugged. "Hell, I don't know. I'll pass that on. What else?"

"She mentioned a Saigon politician with ties to the South's government and to Hanoi. She's speaking with him now to get his position on and requirements for forming a new government."

"That's it?" Jack asked, disconcerted. "What about names of Viet Minh? You know...the commies who are staying in the South... We need those names from her, Charlie."

"Was that part of the plan?"

Jack was silent.

"I thought I was here to assist with a suitable replacement for Prime Minister Diem."

"Of course you are, but..."

"But what?"

Jack sighed, putting his pen down. "Look, for a stable government here to succeed, we must eliminate the Viet Minh leadership. They report directly to Hanoi."

"Ultimately, what difference would that make? I get the strong feeling they'll win anyway. Ho Chi Minh is popular."

"Regardless of what you think, Charlie, our orders are to build a strong stable government in line with American interests. That, my friend, is the mission so do your job, damn it. "

"What exactly are we building that I'm supposed to be part of?"

"A strong anti-communist country." He stood with growing anger. "Or the Chinese will be here and soon all South East Asia will fall."

Charlie shook his head. "You don't know much about the Vietnamese, do you?"

"Don't patronize me." He glared at Charlie.

"I'm the spy and you're my handler. Do I have that right, Jack?"

Jack was done arguing. "Do your job. The one you agreed to do," he said, turned with pad and pen in-hand and left. The door slammed behind him.

That was three days ago, and Charlie had not seen or heard from him since.

Co Vouc handed Charlie a letter from his mailbox. He saw it was from General Stone. He opened it expecting to be fired and sent home. He was mistaken. The general was calling a meeting at his headquarters in two hours.

Since his last conversation with Jack, Charlie had received new information. Diem's soldiers were gathering in the city. They shut down the casino and everyone was deeply concerned trouble was on the horizon. "Much fire. Fire everywhere soon," residents told Truin. "Diem and Vien will fight," she said cautiously. Charlie wondered how much of this the general knew. *Should be a good topic for discussion, anyway,* he decided.

The meeting was well attended. In addition to Charlie and the general were two Americans soldiers, a civilian, and a Vietnamese officer. The latter attendee surprised him.

General Stone introduced the Vietnamese general as General Duc, Prime Minister Diem's Chief of Staff.

"So Major, you have information for us on the current situation in Saigon?" Stone asked to open the meeting.

Charlie related the information Truin had provided him on the massing of government troops in the city.

"What do you think it means?" Stone asked.

"I think it means the Prime Minister is preparing to move on Vien and his soldiers," Charlie replied. "But I think General Duc would know more about that."

"They are gangsters," Duc said. "They must be eliminated."

"How can we allow that group to control the city?" Stone asked. "With fighting erupting in the countryside from forces loyal to Cao Dai and Hoa Hao, the country is coming apart."

"Hell General, this country was never together. Fighting the French gave the various groups a sense of unity they no longer have. Now?" Charlie shrugged. Of the men in the room, Charlie knew he was most circumspect and the only one prepared to give an open, honest opinion to the general.

"We will defeat them," Duc replied forcefully.

"Can you?" Stone asked.

"Yes."

"When?"

"Soon, very soon," Duc said. He abruptly changed the subject. "This woman, Madame Thieu, who your envoy sleeps with, is very dangerous. I think she spies for Hanoi."

"Charlie?"

"She's a business woman here, not a spy. You are mistaken, General," Charlie replied evenly. He had done this drill many times since 1944. He wasn't about to allow anyone push him into a corner, or discuss his personal relationship with Truin. *None of their business,* he decided.

"You know nothing about her," Duc said.

Charlie said nothing. *I know more about her than anyone else in this room,* he thought.

Duc stood and turned to General Stone. "We must speak later, General." He bowed to the others and marched from the room. The Americans watched quietly.

"Shit," General Stone finally said. "We got a problem." He looked to Colonel Archer who had been quiet. "What about the people outside Saigon?"

"We have land reform initiated in February. I think that's a good start. Remember sir, winning here will depend on the support of the farmers who represent 90 percent of the population. We must focus our efforts there. Saigon is a separate problem, with most of the population living outside the city."

Winning? Charlie thought. "Colonel, what does winning look like?" he asked.

"We must gain the support of the peasant farmers to win here," the colonel said.

"Can Diem do it? The general asked.

The colonel shrugged. "I don't know, but who else is there?"

We have three different agendas here. Big problem, Charlie thought. *But I'm just a guest serving at the whim of the CIA.*

"Major?"

"Madame Thieu has a man who she is meeting with as we speak," Charlie replied directly.

"Tell us about him."

His name is Nguyen Xien and he leads the Socialist Party here. His connections with most factions in the South and the North are deep. He could bring a measure of stability until elections are held," Charlie said.

When Charlie mentioned the Socialist Party, the soldiers shook their heads. "Just another commie," the CIA Agent, Barton said, speaking for the others. "Then we might as well give up the country to them."

General Stone listened. "Would Washington accept a socialist?" The question hung in the air.

Charlie already knew the answer.

"Hell no!" Barton said. The others agreed.

"Charlie, when she returns from her meeting, talk to her. Get everything you can on this guy, and get it to me as quickly as you can," the general said, speaking only to Charlie.

"Not a problem, sir."

"Dismissed," Stone announced. "Stay a minute, Charlie. You, too, Barton."

The three waited patiently for the others to file out of the room.

"As we heard here, the woman is in a dangerous spot. We need to move fast," Stone said. "Barton, what's your assessment?"

He paused, obviously searching for an answer. "Well, sir," he began slowly. "Even with the National Front pressing on Diem, the greatest threat in South Vietnam is still the pro-Hanoi supporters, many of whom will stay in the South. They have considerable support among the population. Most importantly, they are well led. Smart, General, smart."

"As you've said before, Barton." He looked at Charlie. "We need intelligence on where the Viet Minh commander, Le Doan, is hiding. "It's your highest priority to get that information from the woman before we lose that asset. She knows him well. That's been long known. Hell, she's probably assisting him."

"That's not why I agreed to come here. I was told that I was an envoy tasked with negotiating with her regarding the Diem government." Charlie stood, angry, again feeling like they had set him up.

"I order you to do what you're told, Major," General Stone replied, growing as angry as Charlie. "Dismissed." He turned and left through the back.

"You want to spend the next ten years like the last, Stanek? Running and hiding from intelligence agencies." Barton growled. "Or you can help us for a few more days and you're home free—with a green card to run your ranch and be left alone. You decide." He walked out the door before Charlie responded.

Son of a bitch knows way too much about me, Charlie thought, brooding.

Charlie and Jack decided to walk back to the Dragon House. "So, what you boys talk about?" Jack asked.

"I need a drink," Charlie replied. "Let's go in here." They turned into a small shanty-type structure. The sudden darkness blinded their eyes. Charlie looked around and spotted bottles lined up on a makeshift counter. "Beer?" Charlie asked an older woman suddenly appearing from the back.

The woman did not understand but nodded.

Charlie picked up a bottle of something that looked local, but he did not care. Warm, he knew, *but I'll drink it anyway.* "Two." He held up two fingers.

They sat on hardwood benches. The woman brought the beer in tall glasses, with a couple of ice cubes in a dish. Charlie drank without the ice.

"You look real pissed, Stanek. They give you a hard time in there?" Jack took a swallow from his glass. "God damned, this beer is boiling hot." He dropped an ice cube in.

"Lying, manipulative bastards," Charlie said, then took a long swallow. "I should have let them deport me from Australia. Now, they got me mixed up in an unfolding, immoral disaster."

"Kind of harsh, ain't ya?"

"You're buddy, Barton, is scum of the earth."

Jack stared at him. "Can't you just do your job? So fucking self-righteous." He shook his head.

Charlie threw the remainder of his beer down in a gulp. "Let's get out of here. I need something stronger. Pay the lady."

They kept walking. Charlie still was not ready to return to Dragon House.

They entered the Intercontinental bar. Charlie looked for the bartender he had met earlier, and found him at the far end of the mahogany. "Two doubles, Four Roses," he shouted.

"Yeah boss," the young man replied and immediately jumped on the order.

They found a table and sat down. The place was deserted. The bartender brought their drinks. He stood there with a smile. "Hard day, boss?" he asked.

Charlie threw his drink down and ordered another. Jack sipped his.

"I spent six years in American intelligence, knew all you assholes including Donovan, and Dulles. Your current boss, right?"

"That's right."

"They dropped me behind German lines in the middle of Central Europe with one other man. Killed by the way. To rescue downed aviators, but mostly I ran patrols with the partisans, fought the Nazis and had to deal with Stalin's NKVD. It was all shit, Jack. War is, but I survived."

"Jack said nothing, just sipped.

"Another round," Charlie waved to the young bartender. "He's probably a commie," Charlie said sarcastically, motioning to the young man, "Better watch him, Jack."

Jack said nothing, continuing to sip his drink.

"Then the general sent me to Indochina. Said it was to investigate a murder, but he set me up. The Russians tortured me, but that's another story. In '48, I went to Czechoslovakia to rescue a woman and her child. You bastards knew about that, too. Washington offered me as bait for a double agent, and again almost got me killed." He took a sip, beginning to slow down. "Now, here I am dealing with you bastards again."

"Write a book," Jack said, sounding indifferent to Charlie's story.

The drinks arrived with a smile.

Jack's comment pissed Charlie off real bad. "Go to hell! You know...You're nothing but some, brain-washed imp," Charlie slurred with growing difficulty. "An ass-kissing Ivy leaguer."

Jack took a sip, and then stood. "Fuck you!" he tossed a hard right into Charlie's face. Charlie went over and out cold. "Never say that," Jack mumbled, "to the Northeast Conference Golden Gloves Champ of 1949."

Of the few guests inside the bar, everyone froze, not knowing how to handle two large Americans fighting. Within minutes, Bob entered, following the bartender.

"No good, no good," Bob said, looking at Jack. He bent down to check Charlie. "We take him back to Dragon House." He waved at two men who ran in and helped move Charlie. "Come, we go," Bob said to Jack. "Back to hotel."

When Charlie woke, he had no idea where he was. A light from the bathroom told him he was in the hotel room but it felt like hell, or worse, one of Pavlov's prisons. He rubbed his temples. "Jeesus, why did I say all that to Jack?" He felt soreness in his cheek, dried blood. "Ouch."

Before he could collect himself, a knock on the door.

"Come in," Charlie called. "It's open."

Jack walked in and sat down. Charlie watched. *At least I know how much he can take of my insults,* he thought. "That's a hard punch, a real haymaker," he said rubbing the swollen area.

"Sorry," Jack replied, "but I'd had enough."

"What do you want?"

"Dinner?"

Charlie stared at him. "Not hungry," he finally replied.

"Ok," he did not move from the chair. "I gave what you said a lot of thought."

"Yeah?"

"Things don't seem like they're working. The reality on the ground keeps changing." He sighed, still sitting. "But what choice do we have here?"

"We always have choices, my friend. Some may not be good, but we still have choices." Charlie was not certain Jack meant them specifically or the U.S. Government.

Jack looked away, at nothing. "Look, the only way we can protect Madame Thieu is to get her out of the country. First, we have to have that information. Tell her that, Major."

Charlie still rubbed his face. The pain in his head thumped. "I'll talk to her," he finally said. "Tonight...later."

Jack stood. "Good. We'll talk in the morning."

"Now, go away." He lay back on the bed.

He lay there until midnight. Slowly, he struggled to the bath, stripped, then stepped into the shower. He stayed there, unmoving, allowing the cold water to pummel him. Slowly, he reinvigorated.

I must talk with her, he thought, dressing. He left the room and took the elevator to the top floor where he knew Truin had her suite. She lived there with her niece.

He knocked, not knowing if anyone would answer. It was one o'clock in the morning. After a single knock, the door opened. Truin stood in the doorway wrapped in a white silk robe decorated with dragons. "Charlie," she said with a smile. "I hear about you. Please come in. We must talk."

"I'm sorry for the late hour," he said, walking in and sitting. Her rooms always seemed to smell fragrant with flowers, but the incense made him feel nauseous. The furniture was lavish, French. He saw that she had been writing. Stationary covered her large bed. Co Vouc was nowhere to be seen.

"You have bad day. Khanh tell me this."

"We must talk about the day, Truin. Things seem to be moving quickly even for Vietnam," he said. "I want to hear of your..."

She bent and kissed him on his bruised cheek. "I love you, Charlie." Her light robe fell open, exposing her naked body. He wrapped his arms around her to pull her close.

They kissed, the robe falling to the floor.

"Come, she said, standing to take his arm.

"We talk first," he said. "It's important for you."

"Yes, we talk." She began slowly undressing him. "I miss you so much today," she said, slowly pulling off each item of clothing and tossing it on the floor. Soon both were naked.

Truin hastily swept the papers from the bed. "When we lay close then we talk," she said, pulling him by the hand to the bed. They lay beside each other.

Charlie knew he was being distracted, and, at-the-moment cared less. He ran his fingers over her body, touching every part of her, while Truin found her pleasure with him.

He lay back and closed his eyes, felt her soothing touch. They made love. After, they relaxed comfortably in the soft bed. She curled up beside him. Charlie was exhausted following a day that seemed never to end, but he knew they had to talk. "Talk to me about the Socialist, Xien," he said rolling onto his side.

"Now we talk." She sat up and smiled, excited. "He will work with the Americans, but only until the elections next year."

Charlie liked hearing that. "Good, I'll inform the general."

"Now we sleep. You very tired, I think."

"One more thing," he said. *The hard part,* he thought. "They want the location of the Viet Minh commander."

"So they can arrest him?" She sat up straight and gave him a hard look.

"Probably," he said. "But if you tell them, they say they will protect you."

"From who?"

"Diem. He wants you, but you already know that." He felt anger building inside her.

"You think I'm so stupid I let him take me?"

"No," he said. "But you have many enemies, and I don't want anything to happen to you."

"Americans," she growled. "They know nothing. What about you, Charlie? What do you think?"

He knew that was coming. "I think you should leave with me. We'll get married, go to Paris."

"No!"

"It's too dangerous here for you."

"Charlie, I want to marry you. I want to..." She held his hand. "But I will never leave my country. Please understand."

"I understand, but..."

"War is dangerous. You know this. We must take many risks," she replied with growing emotion. "Betray my comrades? Never!" She stood and stared at him.

Charlie also stood, held her arms, then thought better of it, and dressed without another word spoken between them.

Before leaving, he looked at her, touched her cheek. "I understand completely, he said, turned and walked out the door. He closed it softly behind him.

The next morning over tea and fruits, Charlie reported to Jack that the socialist was willing to form a temporary government until elections are held.

Jack smiled, but he saw immediately that Charlie was upset. "I'll get that right over to Barton. What about the other?" He was pushing.

Charlie thought long and hard on how he would answer that question. "I'm working on it," he said. "She's still hesitant about divulging anything on the Viet Minh." *Got to buy more time,* he thought. *Fuck these bastards.*

Jack accepted that. He did not want to anger him by prodding him further.

"I have a question for you. Since you're probably not speaking much Chinese here, what are you doing?"

At first, Jack said nothing. "My original assignment with the Agency was to operate a station on Taiwan to monitor radio traffic on the Chinese mainland, but I was replaced, and reassigned to Australia to work with Jon Grey. I like Australia. Nice place."

"You didn't answer my question," Charlie said. "I think you have other skills that Barton is using. What are they?" Since their arrival, he felt Jack's brooding anger, a barely contained violence just beneath the surface. He knew the type, always trying to mask it with their work.

Jack at first struggled with the question, then answered it directly. "I'm setting up a counter-espionage program here."

I suspected as much, Charlie thought. "Interrogation techniques—torture—the whole works, eh?"

"If necessary. You know how that works," he said. "But mostly training Vietnamese soldiers on intelligence gathering, debriefing, that sort of stuff."

"That seems like a difficult job since no American here can speak the language well."

"Not my problem."

"Then you are working closely with General Duc and Diem's National Army? Do I have that right?"

"Yeah, we're developing a relationship."

Charlie liked how he stated that and smiled. "Do the Vietnamese trust you enough to work in a junior role...and share?"

"Not yet, but they will...if they want to hold onto power."

"Good luck," Charlie replied. *At least, I know why he is here,* he thought.

Charlie tried to contact Truin. The days passed, and he did not see her anywhere in the hotel. He asked Co Vouc and she told him only that she has important business at the casino. He worried about how he had left things. He felt caught in the middle between Stone's demands and his loyalty to Truin.

Chapter 7

Saigon, April 27:   The fire everyone fretted over struck the city mid-day. Fighting erupted between Diem's National Army and the Binh Xuyen in the heart of Saigon near Truin and Vien's Grand Monte Casino in the densely populated Cho Lon District. The National Army began their attack with small arms and mortar fire with Vien's men reciprocating in kind. Soon Diem's men resorted to heavy artillery bombardment. By that evening, house-to-house combat engulfed much of the district, while the fires spread through the district, destroying the homes of the poor.

Charlie heard the mortar fire and immediately ran to the balcony. He saw plumes of smoke rise about the Chinese district. *The casino,* he thought. *Where's Truin?* He knew it was just a matter of time before the gangsters and Diem went at it again. He had hoped for more time.

I must find Truin and keep her safe, he decided, running to the door. He hoped she was in her suite, but he really did not know.

He had seen her only once during the past week. They had dinner in the Intercontinental. She asked if they married would Charlie live in Saigon with her, and he had replied that he had to consider his son. *I am a man who has survived being shot at, imprisoned, and tortured. The thought of living in Saigon seemed almost suicidal,* he finally decided. He did not tell her that.

She seemed to understand when he explained the situation with his son. Later they walked hand-in-hand along the Saigon River, admiring the large ships docked there.

Charlie pounded on the door. No answer. He took the elevator to the lobby. He saw Co Vouc and approached her. Just as he reached the desk, soldiers stormed in the front doors. He saw other soldiers spreading out to surround the hotel. An officer stood at the desk in Vouc's face speaking loudly and forcefully.

She looked at Charlie. "No one leave." She sounded very distressed.

"Passports," the officer, who Charlie decided was a captain or major, demanded from Co Vouc.

"Major, they want everyone's passport," she said. "Please obey."

She looked directly at Charlie. "He say that fighting everywhere so he ordered to protect all foreigners."

With Charlie's passports turned over, the major turned to him. "Name?" he asked.

"Charles Stanek, Major, United States Army," he replied.

The officer understood, appearing to recognize Charlie's name. "Where Madame Thieu," he demanded. "You take me."

Fuck you, Charlie thought. "I don't know," he said with a shrug.

"No, you know." The soldier seemed angry.

"No."

The officer turned back to Co Vouc, now speaking to her in a demanding, angry voice.

Trying to intimidate her to get the information, Charlie figured. *They want Truin.*

The major spoke with another soldier standing behind him. The soldier turned to his men.

Vouc looked at Charlie. She was frightened. "They search the hotel for her. He insists you go to your room," she said, fear shaping each word and distorting her young, beautiful features.

Charlie, without speaking, turned for the elevator. Two soldiers followed him. When he entered his room, they stayed at the door. *Protection or house arrest?* Charlie wondered.

He walked to the balcony to look out over the city. He saw smoke billowing from Cho Lon. He heard heavy artillery rounds rumbling overhead, then explosions as they found their targets. He prayed that Truin was somewhere, anywhere outside the city.

Charlie had no doubt that the Americans were somehow involved in this. A perfect foil for American intelligence. He shook his head, knowing things had already changed. He wondered where Jack was. He had not seen him all day, which was unusual.

The battle raged for 48 hours, driving thousands of civilians into the street. In the poor districts, the fighting leveled dozens of buildings, leaving nothing but charred and smoldering ruins behind. Five hundred civilians killed and another 20,000 left homeless.

Diem's soldiers slowly gained the upper hand. Following heavy fighting, Le Grand Monde, which served as Vien's headquarters, overrun by paratroopers and severely damaged. Capture of the casino marked the end of the fighting.

Both sides suffered heavy casualties. More than 300 combatants killed just in the first 24 hours of fighting. By May 2, the battle was over, with Binh Xuyen in full retreat.

The National Army pursued the Binh Xuyen survivors into the countryside and to the Cambodian border. Bay Vien, able to get most of his wealth out of the country, immediately fled to Paris to live the remainder of his life in luxury.

Charlie knew all of this because the guards allowed newspapers delivered to his room, which he greatly appreciated. On the first delivery, someone had attached a note. "Major, courtesy of the *Los Angeles Times*. You owe me a drink." He immediately knew who sent the paper.

Charlie had received no word of Truin. After five days, the city grew quiet again, still she did not show. On the sixth day, there was a knock, and Charlie opened it to find Jack standing there. The guards were suddenly gone.

"Did you win?" Charlie asked. He was not smiling.

"Everything has changed," Jack replied. "The Prime Minister is in firm control here."

"What the hell does that mean?"

"Well...I got you released from custody."

"Should I be grateful?"

"A 'thanks' would be appreciated. They wanted to take you."

"Thanks," Charlie said. "What about Madame Thieu? Where is she? In some torture chamber?"

"I don't know. She seems to have disappeared," Jack said. "I really don't know. Come on. I'll buy you a drink."

"That's it, eh? Where the hell you been for the last week?"

"Jack ignored him. "We'll walk over to the Intercontinental. "I'll try to explain what I know."

They took the elevator to the lobby where Charlie saw Co Vouc for the first time in days. She looked up and smiled at him, without any conversation. Outside, Charlie smelled the air, which reeked of burned rubber, charcoal, diesel, and something else. *Death,* he finally decided. He noticed that Jack had a new bounce to his step.

"Watching them kill each other must do something for your libido, Jack," he said. "You seem pretty chipper this morning."

"I'll be getting the hell out of here soon," he replied. "Back to Australia and my life. You too, buddy."

When did we become buddies? Charlie wondered. "That's what I like—a positive intelligence agent."

The lobby of the Intercontinental was a hotbed of activity when they entered. He saw foreigners everywhere—at the desk, in lines to use the phones, talking and smoking. *Journalists,* he knew. *Who else?* He looked the group over quickly and did not see Betty McCarthy.

The young bartender brought them their usual Four Roses. He sat the drinks down and bowed, smiling broadly.

"Hey, what's your name?" Charlie asked.

"Just call me Joe," the young man said. He turned to serve other customers who were yelling in his ear. Charlie saw that there were many.

"Ok Jack, talk to me."

"Well," he began, and Charlie could already see that he would leave much out. "Diem defeated Xien and his group decisively and now has control over the city. The National Front is no more. Some of his men will probably be absorbed into Diem's army. The rest...who knows. Lots of damage in the city. As usual it's the poor who suffer the most."

"How's General Stone handling this little war?"

"He'll probably be leaving. I heard the President wants a new angle and a new general."

"Diem stays, eh?"

With him firmly in charge, at least around Saigon, I don't think we're going to try to get rid of him."

"Understandable. So what's the next move?"

"For you...and me, I think the situation has changed."

"Does the U.S. Government still want me to work with Madame Thieu?"

"We still want to talk with her, as does Diem. That is, unless she's on her way to Paris with Xien."

"I don't think she left the country. If she's alive, not killed in the fighting, taken by Diem...or you guys, she's around."

Charlie could feel Jack trying to read him.

"Or in the jungle with her buddies," Jack added. "Think you can turn her up for us?"

That confirms the CIA doesn't have her stashed away somewhere, he thought. "I'll find her," he replied, determined. *But I probably will not tell them,* he decided.

Chapter 8

"**H**ey, where's my drink?" A voice said from behind Charlie.

They looked up. "Betty, you survived," Charlie said. "Hey, thanks for the news. I really needed something to read."

Jack was quiet. Finally, he abruptly stood. "Talk to you later, Charlie." He quietly departed the lobby.

"I guess he doesn't like reporters," Charlie said, joking.

"Afraid of us, you mean," Betty said. She sat and pulled out her notebook.

Charlie called Joe over and she ordered a cocktail.

He dropped it off and scurried to another customer.

"You going to interview me?" he asked.

"Maybe. I'm interested in how Americans feel about being trapped in their hotel during social upheaval. Who knows? You may say something interesting."

"Probably not." Charlie sipped his drink.

"Were your frightened Mr. Stanek? Or do I call you Major Stanek?" she asked.

"Charlie." That caught him off guard. "Who told you?"

"I do my homework, and I didn't think a sheep herder would be in Saigon just to visit a friend, a friend as well-known as Madame Thieu. I inquired with General Stone. He explained that you are here as a special envoy to meet with her on issues he said he could not divulge. Top Secret or something like that."

"I telegraphed back to the states after speaking with him, and they dug up some interesting background on you. A war hero, rescuing downed pilots in Central Europe during the war. But you know what, Major? The most interesting, I think, is that there does not appear to be any record of you, except the account that states you were lost at sea in '46. Yet, here you are, alive and well, or so it appears. Man of mystery. Now you're here as a sheep herder from Australia visiting an old friend," she said, proud of herself. "Are you with her now?"

"I've been under house arrest," he replied. "I haven't seen anyone until now."

"Why under house arrest?" She stopped taking notes.

"My friend seems to be persona non grata by Prime Minister Diem. They wanted me to reveal her hiding place."

"Did you?"

"Hell no. I wouldn't tell the bastards even if I knew."

"Madame Thieu..." Betty said, sipping the drink and eyeing Charlie carefully. "And she just happens to be Xien's partner, and we all know what happened to him and his gang."

"Yeah. I didn't see her and I have no idea where she is. She didn't bother to tell me where she was going." Charlie thought a moment, watching Betty sip her cocktail. "You probably know more than I do. You being a reporter and all."

She smiled at hearing that. "Investigative reporter, Charlie," she replied. "I've learned that many people, including the CIA, want to speak with her regarding various matters."

"I've learned that as well." Charlie ordered another round from Joe. "What else?"

"I only know from my sources, she was not involved in the fighting, and probably out in the countryside somewhere."

"Sources? Who are your sources?"

"Charlie, you know a reporter never reveals her sources," she said with a smile. "Thanks for the drink. Now two?" Joe delivered them to the table. "Trying to get me drunk?"

"Just loosening your lips."

"You may be loosening more than that." She smiled while touching his leg lightly.

"Sources?"

"You must know that I will ask for something in return. Information is a valuable commodity here."

"Whatever it is, it's worth it."

"I like how you answered that," she said with a wink. "Charlie, you must get out more."

"I would if I could figure out how."

"Tomorrow. I got an invite to the American compound in Binh Hoa for an interview. Why don't you join me? Give you an opportunity to see more of the country. I even have a car and a driver courtesy of the United States Army."

"You're on." He finished his drink and prepared to leave.

"Not so fast. There's a person here I want you to meet. How's your French?"

"I speak a little. I am a trained linguist, thanks to the University of Chicago and the Army."

"Good," she replied. "Follow me." She stood and pointed with her chin. "A correspondent from *La Monde* is standing alone over there. He's been here a long time and has many contacts."

Betty introduced Charlie to Jacques Chastain. He was not drinking, Charlie noticed immediately. They, at first spoke in French, with Charlie understanding most of the conversation. Then Chastain abruptly changed to flawless English. He looked directly at Charlie when he spoke. "Major, you do not act like the other American soldiers here."

"I'll take that as a complement."

"What is your role?"

Charlie considered how much he should reveal. "I was brought in to negotiate with the various factions, representing Washington. Now I seem adrift. Things have changed so quickly."

Chastain held Charlie's gaze. He felt violated with the Frenchman studying him. "Who have you spoken with, monsieur? I wonder because I think the Americans have so little influence here and understand so little."

"I have spoken with Madame Thieu," he replied, watching him closely for his reaction. He saw the look of surprise on Chastain's face when he mentioned her name. "We know each other from '45."

He sighed. "A lifetime ago, I think," he said finally looking away. "Why did you speak with such a significant person in local politics, eh?" Chastain asked directly.

He's fishing, Charlie decided. "We earlier developed a very personal friendship, and evidently, she now trusted me only to speak with."

"You are CIA?"

"No, U.S. Army."

He nodded. "I see." He thought before continuing. "You know she is Viet Minh, yes?"

"She is many things," Charlie replied. "What's the status of the French Army here?" He asked, quickly changing the subject.

Chastain smiled. "I think they will soon go home. It appears what they want in Indochina is not what your President wants. What's the point in staying? We have lost, no?"

"I get the impression politics has changed since the Prime Minister soundly defeated the National Front factions."

"Not good for your friend, monsieur."

"So what happens now?"

"Good question," he replied. Betty was content to listen. "I think Diem will move quickly to consolidate his hold on the whole country. The South," Chastain said. "You Americans will support this, I think, but General Stone appears to have mixed feelings on whether to back him as their man. The French Army says Diem is weak and unpopular."

"Now the American war."

"Yes," he said. "What will you do, Major? Return to Washington?"

"Australia. I live in Australia," Charlie said.

"Australia? You are a very interesting man, Major. We must talk again while you are still here."

He handed Charlie his card, but for him the conversation was not over. "Where do you think Madame Thieu is, Jacques?" He tried to mask his driving need to know.

Chastain seemed to be pondering the question. "I think if Diem has not captured her...or the Americans, she hides outside the city. Where I do not know, but be assured that everyone looks."

"I've enjoyed our conversation, Monsieur Chastain. I would like to speak with you again." He turned to Betty. "Tomorrow here at the Intercontinental?"

"Tomorrow," she replied. "At 8 sharp. Sleep well." She sounded disappointed.

On the walk back to Dragon House, he considered the conversation with the French correspondent. *There's something he's not telling me,* he thought. *He knew more about Truin than he revealed, or doesn't want the **L.A. Times** to know.*

Entering the lobby, he saw Jack sitting in a far corner.

Jack immediately saw him, motioning him over.

"Hi Jack, waiting for me?" Charlie sat beside him.

"I do not like journalists. Can't control them."

"They can be helpful," Charlie replied. Jack had something to say. Charlie could easily tell. "What's on your mind?"

"Let the woman go, buddy," he whispered. "You tell them you don't know anything, or that she fled to Hanoi. Then you go back to Sydney and sanity."

"What are you worried about?"

Jack stared at him for too long before he spoke. "Things are happening, and if we stay much longer they'll suck us in. It's a deep, dark hole, and I don't want my career destroyed."

"Tell me what you know, Jack. What's changed for the U.S. and for Madame Thieu?"

"I can't," he said, stood, and left the hotel.

Charlie looked up to see Co Vouc motioning for him. He walked to the front desk.

"Major," she whispered. "Later, 10 o'clock come to room. Come alone, No one see. We must talk."

The hour was late. Charlie knocked, and Co Vouc immediately opened the door. "Please Major," she said, motioning for him to enter. He saw that she was dressed for bed, covered in a white robe with dragon imprints.

She must trust me, he thought. Vouc offered him a chair so he sat. "Your message sounded urgent." She wore no make-up and her beautiful features could not mask her worry.

"Truin," she replied. "She has disappeared. No message and that is unusual. Always she tell me."

"Where do you think she is?"

"I do not know. I hope she hides, but I do not know. Soldiers search everywhere," she said, in a voice barely audible. "Soldiers have roadblocks on all roads in and out of Saigon."

"How long has it been since you saw her last?" He tried to make sense out of it.

She paused to think. "Before fire in the city. Maybe 7 days."

That could be a good thing, Charlie thought. "Before the battle?"

"Yes, but Diem has spies everywhere."

"Have you spoken with Khanh?"

"He no see her."

"She has many friends. Could they be hiding her?"

"Truin not in city."

Charlie saw tears streaming down her cheeks. He stood to embrace her. Vouc did not move, but melted into his arms, like a lost and confused child. "Do you think Diem has her?" he asked softly.

"I fear for her life." She did not move from Charlie's arms. "Major, you are good man like Truin say."

"I will find her," he whispered, feeling her pressed against him. He felt needed.

"I will find her with you. She is my aunt and only family left," Vouc said forcefully.

To Charlie, it seemed like she found some inner source of strength. Her tears dried immediately.

"I will ask Khanh to help us," she said. "He knows much."

"Good, tomorrow, I must attend a briefing with the U.S. Army. I will see what they know," he said. *Or are willing to tell me.*

She stepped back from their embrace. She touched his face and smiled. "Thank you. I must know everything so I can help her."

Charlie felt a strong attachment to the young woman, but he was learning quickly. *She has her own agenda, too,* he thought.

Unable to sleep, he lay in the darkness of his room. He wondered what Rusty would say about the people here. This world seemed so different from life in the Outback. Wild, yes, but in a very different way. Here he found no peace of mind, no sanctuary in which to think his thoughts clearly.

Am I so different from the generals, the Americans, the angry factions? Where do the Americans fit in the puzzle if they want peace for this troubled land? Disorder, everywhere disorder. Those thoughts kept flashing through his mind like a neon sign on a late night hotel.

Finally, he slept, but his sleep haunted by a restless presence, of something he could not quite grasp.

Betty was waiting in the Jeep—8 o'clock sharp. *One thing about the army,* he thought. *They're on time.* He jumped in the back.

"Driver, take us by Cho Lon, where the fighting occurred," she urged.

"But..." he said, hesitating. "Ok, why not?" He had a quick change of mind.

They extinguished the fires that swept the area, but smoke and the charred remains of buildings were everywhere. Charlie saw people already trying to rebuild.

"What will they do now?" Betty asked. "Will you help them rebuild?"

The driver, a staff sergeant, shrugged. "Not our problem."

"But there are thousands left homeless," Betty argued.

The sergeant looked at her while shifting. "Do I look like a construction worker? We're advisors here only."

Betty was writing as they drove through the carnage. Charlie saw a badly damaged casino. "I'll bet that gets rebuilt quickly, Sarge," he quipped.

Sarge laughed. "Money talks, sir. You know that."

Diem's soldiers were everywhere

"Can we stop? Only for a moment," Betty said, prepared to get out of the vehicle.

Sarge thought about it, shrugged, and pulled over beside a group of soldiers. "Can you speak the lingo?" he asked.

"A little," she said excited. "I've been here awhile." Betty walked over to the soldiers and began speaking in halting Vietnamese.

The officer in charge replied. The other soldiers tried to listen in. The Americans understood hardly a word.

The soldier shook his head in a definitive way. He seemed very unpleasant.

Betty turned to return to the Jeep.

"Learn anything?" Charlie asked.

"He said we won a great victory for Vietnam," she replied. "But what he said next really annoyed me."

"What's that?"

"All foreigners must get out of Vietnam now."

They continued their drive to Binh Hoa. It was uneventful, bouncing along through large puddles and potholes in the Jeep with its tight suspension. Charlie was relieved when they finally arrived. They entered through a gate and for the first time, he saw dozens of Americans in uniform walking about. The jeep stopped in front of a large French villa. "This is the place," Sarge announced. "I'll wait for you outside. Just yell when you're ready." Betty and Charlie got out and entered the building.

Another enlisted man ushered them into a large room with many folding chairs arranged in rows. *Must be a briefing room,* Charlie thought, as they made their way to the front of the drab room. Half-dozen reporters representing other news organizations filed in after them.

"The colonel will be here shortly," the sergeant announced, turned and left.

"Where's the general?" Charlie asked him.

No reply.

Within a few minutes, Colonel Archer entered the room. "Welcome," he said, directing his attention to Betty in the front row. "I'm Colonel Anthony Archer, heading up the Saigon Military Mission."

"Which is?" Betty, with pen and notebook in hand, asked.

"Excellent question. Miss? Miss?"

"Betty McCarthy, *Los Angeles Times.*

"Yes, Miss McCarthy," Archer said. "Good question. My primary role here as an advisor is to undertake paramilitary missions and train South Vietnamese soldiers in psychological warfare. The American mission here consists of about 350 men."

Charlie listened.

"How's that working, Colonel? Your mission...?" Another reporter asked, sitting immediately behind them. Charlie turned to notice the man was with the *New York Times*.

"We are working with Vietnamese at all levels of the military structure from the National Army to local force units. I think it is very important to the success of the Government here that we, they gain the support of the people. It's kind of a hearts and minds type of operation. We must compete in every village for their support."

"Sounds like a tough job," A voice from the rear of the room called. "How do you do that?"

"Of course, with only 350 men, we cannot do it alone. Therefore, we must train Vietnamese to engage them. Their people, after all." Charlie could tell the colonel was trying for witty, but it fell flat. No one even smiled.

"Finally, Charlie had enough of the party line. He stood to ask a question. "Colonel, where is General Stone this morning?"

Archer stared at him. "Major Stanek," he said slowly and dryly. "The general could not be with us. He is, well, he is indisposed."

"I bet," Charlie replied.

Ignoring him, Archer focused again on Betty. "Any questions thus far?"

"Please excuse me." Charlie prepared to leave.

Questions from around the room bombarded Archer as Charlie walked out the door.

Charlie was waiting in the Jeep when Betty came out of the building.

"Learn anything you didn't already know?" he asked Betty as she got in.

"Nope." She turned to the driver. "Sergeant, can we drive around the compound. I would like to see the men. You know...talk to the young Americans. For a human interest story I'm doing."

"Not a problem," the driver replied.

Seeing several GIs standing around a water cooler, Betty motioned for the driver to stop. She got out, walked over and introduced herself. Charlie could tell they were opening up to her. Soon a good dialogue developed between her and the young soldiers.

"Have you seen any type of action?" she asked.

"No," a young sergeant with a Texas drawl replied. "But got shot at a couple of times."

"Have you run into any Viet Minh soldiers?"

"The Vietnamese soldiers here are interrogating a couple they brought in after the fighting, along with others."

"A patrol was ambushed last night just outside the gates here," an older soldier said. "They suspect Viet Minh."

"Why aren't the Viet Minh going north? Betty asked. "I thought there was some type of truce so they could go north."

"Good question," the sergeant replied.

Charlie stood beside her, listening quietly.

"What have you found in the villages?" Betty asked. "Are you training the local militias? The colonel said that was your mission."

They looked at each other. "We are," an older staff sergeant said finally. "But, like everything here, it's not that easy. They are fearful of us; don't trust the Viet Army or us. It's been difficult to build any trust."

Betty wrote everything down. She looked up at the older sergeant, the highest ranking of them, she guessed. "The colonel said I could accompany you when you visit a village."

The sergeant smiled. "Yes, ma'am, we could use the company."

"Now, I would like each one of you to tell me your name and hometown, then say a few words for the folks back home. Will you do that for me?"

They each agreed.

After completing the interviews, she thanked them.

Before they got in the Jeep, Charlie called out a question. "Where do the Vietnamese soldiers hold their captives?"

"The next compound over. They have a holding area. It's a large empty room, no furniture, nothing. They've been throwing prisoners in there after the fighting in Saigon," the staff sergeant said. "I can take you over to their compound."

"I appreciate that," Charlie said. The three got in the Jeep and the driver roared through the gate and across the road. The staff flashed his badge and the guard allowed entrance. At the holding area, the Vietnamese guard greeted them.

With the staff sergeant and his limited language skills trying to translate, Charlie explained that he was an envoy of the U.S. Government and he wanted to see the prisoners. At first, the Vietnamese guard was hesitant, and then he called a higher-ranking officer over to confer with regarding their request. Finally, that officer motioned for them to follow.

Following two Vietnamese soldiers, Charlie, Betty, and the American sergeant slowly walked the length of the room. The prisoners yelled and jeered while they walked through the rows of prisoners. They were shackled, most sitting or lying on the damp floor. The filth was everywhere and he saw very little fresh water for them to drink. Charlie saw that the women were as numerous as the men, but no Truin.

"I look for Madame Thieu," he said as they walked back to the entrance. "Do you know of her?"

"Madame Thieu? The officer repeated. "No."

"Ask him if this is the only prison," Charlie asked the American sergeant.

The sergeant in halting Vietnamese, relying on gestures, asked the officer.

The officer turned to Charlie. "Not here, sir," he said. "We keep high ranking prisoners in Saigon jail. Look there."

"What will happen to them?" Betty asked with growing concern.

The soldier shrugged.

"Are they being tortured?" she pressed.

The American sergeant frowned. The Vietnamese guard looked at her indifferent, but did not respond.

"They have their own way of extracting information," the American said, demonstrating his way of circumventing the question.

"Did you get enough for your story?" Charlie asked after dropping the sergeant off.

"Pretty much," she replied. "Not much seems to be happening, at least for the American soldiers. I was told they are expecting and hoping for more troops to arrive this year."

"Now the American war begins," he said. "Right now, I think most of the action is at a higher level of command, like who will run the country until elections are held."

"I think you're right. We can probably find General Stone at the bar, his usual hang out," she said. "I'll see if I can get us an interview."

"Now that the casino is closed, he may be at the Intercontinental," Charlie said.

"No Madame Thieu. Sorry about that, Major," she said. "Going to pay a visit to the Saigon jail?"

"I have to."

"Sounds unpleasant. Good luck there."

They got out at the Intercontinental. As he was entering, Charlie spotted Bob.

"Hey Bob," he called with a wave.

Bob saw him and approached. "Where to, Major?"

"Saigon Jail."

Bob stared at him. "Bad place, very bad," he said. "Why?"

"It's possible Madame Thieu may be held there. We have to find out.""

"Ok, we go."

At a checkpoint, two MPs waved them down. One of them walked toward the driver's window. He spoke with Bob.

"He say no enter. I ask about Madame Thieu and he say not here. Her very important. They take to Presidential Palace."

"Then to the palace."

Two security police officers stopped them at a roadblock near the Palace gate, one of several roadblocks, but the first two they easily passed through. "Bob, tell them I am a special envoy of the President of the United States. I must speak to General Duc about a woman in his custody."

Bob explained to the guard who looked closely at Charlie. Bob got out of the Citroen.

"Step out," he say."

"Papers please," the guard said. Charlie noticed that at each stop the ranking officer's grade grew. Now he was speaking with a major.

"Papers no good," the officer said. "Must have American general's signature. Must get."

Bob watched, shaking his head.

"I want Madame Thieu. Do you know her?"

"Yes, I know," he said. "Go...now."

Bob turned the Citroen around and they left.

"If she's there, how do we spring her, Bob?

"Spring her?"

"Free her," Charlie said.

Bob shrugged. "I don't know."

Chapter 9

Failing to enter the palace grounds, Charlie and Bob returned to the Intercontinental, without any useable information on Truin's location. He thanked Bob and entered the hotel. He hoped the general was in the bar but he doubted it very much. Unlike the day before, the lobby was deserted, and looking around, he saw few people in the bar.

"Hey Joe, a double," he called to the bartender.

"A damn mystery," he mumbled to himself.

"Major, I wondered when you'd show," a voice said.

Charlie turned and saw Betty. He smiled. "I see you didn't wait."

Holding a drink, she got up and walked over to the bar to get closer to Charlie. "You're writing a good story for me. 'American searching for his Vietnamese lover amid the turbulence of Saigon,'" Betty said, setting her drink down.

Joe delivered Charlie's drink, but continued to stand near them.

"Kind of melodramatic, aren't you?" Charlie said, noting Joe's interest.

She smiled. "Maybe."

"It's a crazy place, ain't it? How have you survived for this long?" he asked. "No lover to keep you sane here?"

"They're too short," she replied. "And I don't screw colleagues. But I like Australians or whatever you call yourself."

"I like Australian," he replied. "Hey, how about dinner somewhere? You must know all the good places to eat."

"I got a better idea. Why don't you come up to my room and we'll order in."

"Sounds like a good idea. I don't see General Stone around," he said.

They finished their drinks and left the bar.

Betty's room was on the top floor and very basic, not like his accommodations in the Dragon House. Newsprint from various papers littered the chairs. He saw notebooks stacked on a bedside table. Upon entering the room, she immediately went to the bathroom, leaving Charlie sitting on the bed.

"Anything interesting come up you can share with me?" he asked, through the door.

"No," she replied. A few minutes later, she returned in a robe. She walked around the bed as if trying to decide something, then stopped to stand in front of him. Her robe fell open to reveal a glimpse of a nude body. "I think we need a distraction," she stated matter a fact. She sounded all business.

Charlie smiled while admiring her. "I think you're right." He stood and nudged the robe with his fingers. It fell to the floor. He admired the fullness of her figure, her firm breasts. She was not a short person, but tall, slender and very muscular. He had grown used to seeing her in khakis and a baggy safari shirt. "I think I like female reporters," he said.

"We're a special breed," she whispered, and began to undress him, starting with his trousers. Soon both were naked.

Holding her breasts in his hands, he kissed one then the other while she fondled him.

"Am I too bold for an Australian sheepherder?" she asked.

"You are," he said, placing his fingers on her abdomen, softly rubbing her soft skin.

Enjoying his touch, Betty nudged him and they fell on the bed, her on top. "I can see you're a man who enjoys distractions."

They made love and, for both, it was a release—her from her lonely and demanding work and him because of a frustrating and failed search for Truin.

They lay in bed the remainder of the afternoon, Betty providing a comprehensive review of world affairs. Finally, Charlie tired of the talk—mostly one-sided. Growing more restless, he readied to leave.

"I'm going," he said, then turned to kiss Betty on the cheek. "Thanks for the fun. Probably see you tomorrow." They never ordered dinner, but he did not care.

His suddenness surprised her. "Enough of world affairs, eh?" She rolled on her side to watch him dress.

"I have to find out what my status here is. I could be asked to leave or even deported." He dressed hurriedly.

"It's kind of late. Who you going to ask at this hour?"

Charlie smiled. "Jack, of course."

"Who the hell is Jack?"

Jack is assigned to me as an assistant," Charlie replied. "But more like my handler. It's the CIA after all. I really don't know what else he's up to here." He shrugged.

"I don't want to hear anymore."

"Betty, you hear anything, anything at all, about Madame Thieu, let me know."

"Not giving up, are you?"

"I feel responsible for her safety...and she is an old friend."

"You going to steal her away to your sheep ranch?"

"Station. It's a sheep station," Charlie corrected. "Probably not."

Taking a slow stroll back to the Dragon House, a man stepped out of the shadows to greet him. He was dressed in dark clothing that blended into the darkness and obscured his identity.

"You look for Madame Thieu?" he asked in barely understandable English.

"Who told you?" The man's sudden appearance surprised Charlie, but he held his ground, seeing the man was not armed.

"Spies everywhere. Hear foreign people talk."

"What do you want?"

"You pay for information?"

"For good information."

"I have," he replied. "Give me American dollars."

Charlie pulled the folded bills from his pocket. "This is all I have."

The man swiped them out of Charlie's hand and examined them. "Ok," he said. "Madame Thieu go see Bao Dai, see Emperor, before fight. I know. I see her. They take her north."

"Where? Hue?"

"No Hue. Into mountains. DaLat."

"Where is she now?" Charlie asked. "Tell me."

"I don't know," he said. "No see her again. I look but she disappear." He stepped back into the shadows as suddenly as he came and was gone.

Charlie stood at the door to the hotel. *Just before the battle started, I knew where she was. But afterward?* And that's what worried him the most.

He took the elevator to his room, but stopped at Jack's door. *CIA agents never sleep,* he decided, and knocked.

Jack was sleeping which surprised him. "Jack, what's our status here? Are we being sent back to Australia?" he asked as soon as the door opened to a groggy, half-asleep CIA agent.

"Come in," he said.

Charlie entered and closed the door. He watched as Jack quickly collected himself.

"Our status has not changed, so you still have a couple of days to find your Viet Minh lover," he said but not sarcastically.

Charlie sat down. "I'm striking out," he replied.

"It's a big country, eh? Especially when you search for one person."

"What's going on here? Do we support Diem or not?"

Jack shrugged with apparent indifference. "Shake up with the American command. No one has seen General Stone lately. I think Washington wants someone else." He still stood facing Charlie. He watched him groggily, still half-asleep.

"Who?"

He finally sat down across from Charlie. "Hell, I don't know. They don't tell me."

"Hey, you're the CIA. You must know something."

Jack considered. Charlie knew he was deciding what he could share. "Ok, consider this: Madame Thieu met with Bao Dai."

"I already know that."

Of course you do," Jack replied. "Also, she wasn't there long. Before we could apprehend her, she took off, right from under our fingertips. The woman is good, Charlie. Where? We have no idea. Diem's men were there, too. They may have her, or she managed to escape them, too. I asked but no one told us anything."

"She just disappeared?" Charlie asked, confused. Isn't Bao Dai in DaLat? That's in the mountains north of here. You were there?" He already knew the answer, but he wanted to discover whether Jack would tell him the truth.

"You're right. He's in DaLat, and not that far. Barton said it was a summer residence. We drove up and back the same day without incident. Barton suspects she went into the mountains to hide"

"You drove to DaLat to apprehend her?"

"Better us than Diem and his boys."

"You have safer, cleaner interrogation methods, right?"

"Not like that."

"You get around, Jack. Here I just thought you were sleeping and enjoying the sunshine. Now I discover you've been spying," Charlie said flatly. "Earning your pay, eh?"

"We consider her very important. Barton wants the Viet Minh commander real bad. Dead or alive, so as you can understand, it's top priority," Jack said, trying to defend their actions. "We'll give her back to you when we're done."

"Thanks, you bastard."

"Get with the program, Major."

"But you failed to get her?" *He is not telling me everything.* "I think you boys need to hire me for the job," he said, frustrated.

"We already have," Jack said. "So get on it."

"I need to know everything you know, so tell me."

"I already gave you everything you're going to get," Jack replied. "Use your sources and keep me posted. But I must caution you, Charlie. We now consider the woman a commie spy, an asset of Ho Chi Minh. Remember that."

Charlie remembered what Truin had told him those many years ago. *"I serve Ho Chi Minh proudly like you serve President Truman,"* she said simply.

Jack is trying to keep me occupied and out of his way, he decided. Everything is a lie.

Why should I tell him anything? Charlie thought, walking back to his room. *My sources? Bob, who's not much help thus far. There is nothing more I can do if Diem has her. However, if she is free, Bob must know how to find her...I hope.*

DaLat? Charlie considered. *DaLat, a city of beauty and peacefulness, she said.* He remembered the city from ten years ago. High in the Lam Vien Highland they had traveled to the DaLat Hill Resort built by the French. *We were hunting the Japanese war criminal, Captain Suzuki, who we chased to an abandoned prison camp at a place called Plei Toan. At the camp during the final year of the war, Suzuki summarily executed American aviators held as POWs.* Charlie would never forget that trip.

He considered his conversation with Jack. *I have to assume the Vietnamese notified the CIA about Truin's presence in DaLat. There is a very good chance either the Vietnamese or the CIA have her already, which Jack would never divulge to me. This was their plan all along.*

The bastards, he fumed, believing Jack had betrayed him.

Chapter 10

Charlie lay in bed, where he did his best thinking. Sleep seemed impossible and the hours ticked by. The constant rhythmic hum of the ceiling fan positioned directly over his head no longer disturbed him. He had opened the balcony door wide for more air, but now had to listen to the street noise outside. Suddenly, an idea possessed him. He sprang from bed, dressed, and left the room. He had no regard for time but knew it was very late...early in the morning. Avoiding the elevator, he took the stairs up two at a time to the top floor.

He knocked hard several times. Finally, he heard movement.

"Who?" a woman's voice asked in Vietnamese.

"Charlie. We must talk. Very important," he said through the door.

The door slowly opened and Charlie rushed in. "Co Vouc," he said, turning to face her, as she emerged from behind the door. He saw that she was barely dressed, and had haphazardly pulled her robe together, exposing a small breast.

"Major?" Her voice was calm, like she was pleased to see him.

She was expecting me, he thought, confused. "Sorry," he said, "but it's very important."

"Come. Sit," she said, covering herself by drawing the cord tighter. Yet, she appeared not to be embarrassed. "I've been waiting. You have information on Truin?"

"Not to confuse you, but I have information on where she isn't," he replied. "Let me explain." He related the events of the last 24 hours and what he had learned.

When he was finished, she stood and walked to the window to look out over her city. At first, she said nothing. "Bao Dai did not help her. He is a coward, only in his position as President because of the French and you Americans. Yes, Charlie, you are correct. If the Prime Minister holds her there is little we can do unless the American Army assists." She turned to look at Charlie. "I have better news. General Duc still searches for her, which means Diem does not have her...yet. His men everywhere in hotel. Today he does this. Look."

Charlie saw clothing still scattered about the floor, but neatly scattered with clothing folded in neat piles. *That's strange.* "Where do you think she is? In the delta?" he asked

"No, too far and too dangerous. Still much fighting there," Vouc said, sitting beside him. She touched his hand and sighed. "Too many roadblocks."

"She was in DaLat to visit Bao Dai," he said. It's very possible that she is hiding in the mountains. Any ideas where?"

"As a child, I spent much time there. Such a beautiful place," Vouc said. "Truin knows the area well and the people."

Charlie watched her, thinking about a next step. "I think we must go there. Have Khanh drive us. We may get lucky?"

"Get lucky?"

"A term for having success."

She smiled. "Yes, get lucky," she repeated. "Tomorrow very early we go to Da Lat. I send message to Khanh. Ok, good."

Returning by the stairs to his room, something suddenly occurred to Charlie, something he found very disconcerting. *Why does she know so much about the Army's movements but nothing about Truin's location? Vouc is the one person Truin confides in, yet she is clueless about her whereabouts.* "Vouc, are you playing games with me?" he asked himself. "Are you really with me?" He reached his room and opened the door. *Did soldiers ransack her room or did she do it herself wanting me to think they did. She waited up for me knowing I would come.*

Khanh was knocking on Charlie's door bright and early at 7:30, forcing Charlie to get up. "Yeah," he said, opening the door to the Vietnamese cabby.

"Hurry, we go. Vouc in car already."

"Give me about 20 minutes and I'll be down," he said.

Charlie walked out of the lobby into the bright sunshine carrying a ceramic cup with tea. Khanh and Co Vouc from the backseat watched him quietly from inside the Citroen. Khanh jumped out to open the passenger door. "We go," he said, slamming the car door behind Charlie.

"Good morning," Charlie said, trying for pleasant, but failing.

However, the two Vietnamese smiled and nodded anyway.

Charlie looked back at Vouc. Dressed in black silk pajama-like bottoms and a khaki top, he decided she was dressed for the trip. "You look lovely this morning," he said to her.

Vouc blushed. "Thank you, Major," she said.

"What can we expect on the drive, Bob?" Charlie asked.

"Roads not good and roadblocks. Army watches everyone."

The last time I made this trip, I was heavily armed. Now, nothing. That thought concerned him but he said nothing.

They moved quickly through the city. Within a short distance, they came upon their first roadblock. Charlie pulled his papers from a shirt pocket. He was prepared. Two soldiers came to the driver's window and spoke with Khanh.

"We must get out," he said, repeating the order.

"No," Vouc ordered them. "I will take care of it." She exited the backseat, said a few words to the guard. The soldier nodded and rushed back to a senior officer. Vouc continued to stand beside the car. To Charlie she did not seem upset, or concerned, but projected a peaceful presence. When the officer approached, she smiled and bowed. They spoke, both in pleasant conversational tones. Finally, Vouc turned to Khanh. "We go." The officer wrote something on a small slip of paper and handed it to Vouc.

"She got back in the Citroen. "We have no more problems. We have pass to DaLat."

Charlie was impressed. "What did you tell him?"

"I know the general well."

Too well, he thought, suspecting she already knew they held Truin in DaLat. "You are very clever," Charlie whispered but she did not hear.

The trip was uneventful and they reached the mountains quickly. They ran into two more roadblocks but the pass got them through immediately. They stopped several times for water, but still made good time.

Arriving at the old French resort before midday, Bob stayed with the car while Charlie and Vouc entered the lobby. They walked to the front desk, Charlie following her lead. He was impressed yet suspicious of the self-confidence and poise she displayed on the trip.

Charlie casually scanned the beautifully constructed hotel and thought that it had not really changed from ten years ago. That night long ago he spent was unforgettable for him. He was bludgeoned over the head in one of the rooms, and somehow whisked away to Hanoi, where he woke days later, shackled to the floor in the old French prison. He could thank Russian intelligence and Colonel Pavlov for his kidnapping.

I wonder what we will encounter on this trip, he thought, preparing for anything.

The general will see us in his room," Vouc said, turning to Charlie.

When they entered his room, they immediately found themselves surrounded by soldiers. Charlie recognized General Duc from their earlier meeting. "General," he said walking over to offer his hand.

The general took it and then bowed. "Major," he said. "We meet again."

"Yes, General Duc," Charlie replied. "I hope you can help us. I must speak with Madame Thieu on behalf of General Stone." Vouc stood beside Charlie.

"General Stone? He is gone, Major."

That surprised Charlie. He knew a decision to replace him was very recent.

"A new representative from your government should arrive soon, I think," the general said. "So, it seems you represent no one at the moment."

"My mission has not changed. I wish to speak with Madame Thieu." Charlie knew he had to be persistent.

The general found that amusing. "I'm sorry, Major. It seems everyone wants to speak with her. Other Americans were here yesterday for the same reason, but she is gone. You have made the trip for nothing, I fear."

"Where has she gone? Her niece is searching as well."

"Tea?" he asked Vouc. "Major?"

"Thank you," Charlie replied graciously.

"Please sit and we will talk."

Charlie saw that he was most interested in speaking with Vouc. A soldier brought tea.

"I think Madame Thieu has many friends here, some who hide her, but we will find her. I know the Prime Minister wishes to speak with her...and Major, I'm afraid he has priority. Perhaps, you will help us?"

"We may both want to speak to her, but I think for different reasons."

The general began speaking with Vouc in Vietnamese, initiating a conversation about what Charlie had no idea. He looked at her inquisitively.

"I go to school with General Duc's son," she said to Charlie, anticipating his question.

"That is so," the general said, smiling at her. "My son is now living in Paris, where I think you should go. So much trouble here for one so young and beautiful. It is too late, I fear, for your aunt."

Charlie said nothing, but the last comment concerned him. *A warning or a threat? Did he already have her?*

"Soon the Prime Minister will settle things. Soon."

I wonder what that means, Charlie thought.

Charlie was relieved to be away from General Duc and back in the Citroen. "Now what?" he asked.

"I think south to Duc Trong," Vouc said. "I know of a man there who can help us."

They were soon on a highway that was hardly a two-lane trail. The mountains and jungle surrounded them. Charlie wished he was armed, but no soldiers bothered them. He decided the National Army did not control the road they were taking. He saw no roadblocks or soldiers anywhere.

"You are very well-connected," Charlie said to Vouc. "Tell me about that."

"Among the elite in Vietnam, we know each other well."

"How well?" *So arrogant,* he thought, surprised she would say that

"We friends, only friends," she replied.

"Yeah," Charlie said. "Did General Duc say more about Truin in your conversation?"

"She was in DaLat yesterday, then escape, he say. Too many friends and the President does not care."

"How long has the general been in DaLat?"

She shrugged. "He is head of Army," was her short reply.

"What did you study at university?" A change of conversation was necessary and Charlie needed to know more about this young woman.

"Music," she said with a smile. "But I had to learn politics. In my family that was very important."

"Your family?"

"My father died when I was very young. My mother and brother died during the war with the Japanese. I have one brother who lives. He is in Paris, I think. That is all my family except for Truin. She raised me and taught me about life."

"I'll bet she did," Charlie replied. "Music?"

"I play traditional Vietnamese folk music...and jazz." She laughed. "I sing and play piano, too."

"What do you believe, Vouc? I mean about your country?"

"Like everyone, I wish for peace and I believe in de-moc-racy. Truin has told me much about your country...and you, Major."

"Charlie, please call me Charlie."

"Charlie."

"Did Truin talk to you about her service with the Viet Minh?"

"No."

"Why not, since you were so close to her."

Vouc shrugged. "Only her business. She say she want to protect me, but..."

She does not trust you, he thought, finishing her sentence.

They approached a very large village. Entering, they passed a small compound with a high guard tower. He saw armed men around its parameter.

"Duc Trong," Bob said. Vouc directed him through the village.

Finally, they pulled up in front of a small pagoda. "Come," Vouc said to Charlie. "I will introduce you to a family friend."

"I will stay with the car," Bob said.

Charlie and Vouc entered. Vouc took his hand and led them to an altar. "We do," she said, lighting incense in front of well-worn photos. Pointing to the largest middle photo, she said, "Ong Duc Truk was a great master, Charlie."

Looking around the small area, he saw photos of Bao Dai and even one of Ho Chi Minh.

From the shadows, an older man with shaved head and dressed in an orange robe approached them. Vouc turned and immediately bowed to the older man, who to Charlie, seemed ancient. They spoke softly. Finally, the man motioned for them to follow.

They were in a small garden behind the pagoda. He motioned for them to sit, and ordered tea be brought from a young man also dressed similarly. *A novice,* Charlie decided. The monk and Vouc spoke softly with Vouc holding his hand and nodding. Charlie sat quietly all the while the two spoke. *Buddhists,* he thought, *another group who want power in Vietnam. I wonder who they support.*

"I tell him you are a friend...and Truin's lover."

"Friend," Charlie corrected. "Tell him I am only a friend." He sipped the tea impatiently.

She smiled, but it was more a look of satisfaction. "Friend," Vouc said nodding her approval.

"Has he seen her?" Charlie asked.

"Yes," Vouc said excited.

The monk again spoke only to Vouc.

"He asked if I would sing for him."

The monk called and four young monks entered the garden. He spoke to them and they sat. Vouc stood and bowed to the gathered monks. She began to sing what Charlie believed was a Vietnamese folk song. The young men closed their eyes. Her soft melodic voice floated through the garden like a soft breeze. Even Charlie began to relax. Vouc saw him leaning back in his chair, and slowly moved to stand beside him.

The old monk saw this and smiled. When she finished, she bowed and everyone smiled. She sat again beside Charlie.

The monk spoke.

"What did he say?" Charlie asked.

"He say, 'the Gods have spoken, and revealed our destiny together."

"What does that mean?" He was reminded of Rusty and his Aborigine people.

"I don't know," she replied, and asked the monk to explain.

He did and Vouc translated. "I feel your energy, foreigner, but I also see a darkness about you that will one day smother your spirit. Yes, danger surrounds you. If Vouc is near, she must protect herself. The Communists are very dangerous."

Charlie noticed immediately that the old man had frightened Vouc. He had no time for Buddhist fortune telling. "Tell him that we must find Madame Thieu before she is harmed."

When Vouc translated, the monk laughed.

"'Her destiny is different from ours,' he say."

"Vouc, we must know."

She translated while listening to the old man.

"He say two American soldiers with Vietnamese soldiers come yesterday. They learn Madame Thieu comes here in old car with others, so they search for her."

"Where did she go?" Charlie saw the old monk more of a politician for his own cause than a peaceful man intent on filling his day meditating. *Not like the Aborigines,* he quickly decided. He also saw that he thought very highly of Vouc and not so much of Americans.

"He doesn't know, Charlie, but thinks Americans capture her before she leave village. Americans here. Talk with them, he say."

"Then we have to go to the compound we saw earlier."

"Yes, Charlie. He say one more thing. 'She send message with young boy from village, and he runs into the jungle.' I think she sends for others," Vouc said.

Charlie stood immediately upon hearing that. "Let's go."

"Soon you will learn much about betrayal," the old monk said in French, looking directly at Charlie. Vouc frowned, but did not translate for him. She did not have to.

Charlie understood. *It was meant only for me.*" An interesting aside, or warning, perhaps, and he seems to know the young woman well.

For Charlie, the pieces were fitting together. *The soldiers at the hotel never ransacked Vouc's room. They already knew where she was, as did Vouc. Hmm.*

The old Citroen entered the compound at the edge of the village. A crudely constructed tower stood beside a barbed wire gate with two soldiers inside standing guard. A dirt berm surrounded the compound with sandbagged firing positions spaced out along its stretch. Two buildings, partially sandbagged, stood inside the parameter. One was an older one-story house with a small heavy block building off to the side. *An armory,* Charlie decided. The other, a much cruder, bamboo and tin structure, appeared to be a barracks.

Seeing an American Jeep parked in front of an old French style building, Bob parked beside it.

Charlie got out quickly and entered. He saw a U.S. Army staff sergeant standing in the middle of the room and approached him. "Sarge," he said. "You have a female prisoner here?"

"Who wants to know?" he asked.

"Major Charles Stanek, sent by Major Barton to pick up a female prisoner. Is she ready to travel to Saigon?"

"We picked her up in the village yesterday. We had her description and were on the lookout. We caught her trying to flee into the jungle," he replied. "Hey, you guys are fast, but you don't communicate very well. Less than four hours after we called it in, two Americans in civilian clothes with a Vietnamese officer picked her up. I was impressed. She must be important," he said.

A dozen Vietnamese were practice firing their M-1s along the berm. The noise was distracting. "With the roads here, I figured we'd have to hold her for at least a couple of days," the staff sergeant said, his voice raised above the gunfire.

"She's gone?" Charlie looked at Vouc. "We'll return to DaLat, talk to the general again."

"He lie to us, Charlie. No reason to speak again with him."

"Yeah? That was a long conversation you had with General Duc. You thought she was still there when we arrived, didn't you?"

Vouc did not answer.

Suddenly, dark heavy clouds opened up and a downpour forced everyone indoors except Khanh who stayed in the Citroen.

"Hey Mac," the staff sergeant called to the other American. "They want the woman, too." He turned to Charlie. "She was a very nice looking woman and spoke English. The two Americans--civilians...one man said his name was Barton, said she was a Viet Minh spy. He showed me his orders. They arrived in a truck filled with Vietnamese soldiers. He said we shouldn't tell anyone, but I figure you intelligence boys all work together. Right?"

Charlie said nothing, content to watch the rain pounding into the red dirt. *Who has her at the resort? The Vietnamese or the Americans?* Charlie was perplexed.

The rain gradually diminished.

"It'll be dark soon. You going to take a chance on going to Saigon or stay the night. I could use some company, someone who speaks English. We've been out here working with them for more than a week."

"Sorry, we got to get back."

They both watched a steady stream of water flow through the compound.

"Not on this road, you're not. Nothing but mud now," Sarge said. "Probably impassable in that car at least until morning. So I guess you are my house guests."

Chapter 11

Charlie spoke at great length with the two American soldiers, but mostly with Staff Sergeant Ricardo Ramirez who was in charge. He learned that he was a career soldier from El Paso, Texas, and married with children. He had fought in Korea and was enjoying his tour here in Indochina. He told Charlie he did not really understand the politics but as a soldier, he could focus primarily on his mission—to train paramilitary to defend their hamlets from any outside attack.

The night passed. Co Vouc slept in an empty room where they had confined Truin, but Khanh chose to sleep in his car. Ramirez had posted sentries. He and his sergeant—Robert Miller, Chicago, Illinois, rotated shifts. Charlie saw that their men were lightly armed with American rifles and one French machine gun.

Charlie grew tired and decided to retire to the room Vouc slept in. He found a sheet of canvass and lay down. Soon, he was dozing off. He heard a noise, opened one eye then the other. Co Vouc had moved from her spot and was trying to lie against him. Surprised, he put his arm around her to pull her close, but he had growing suspicions about where her loyalties lie. The old monk said betrayed? He considered that, but said nothing, knowing she would probably lie to him again.

Curled up in his arms, pressing her body close to his, she fell asleep.

He hoped it was a matter of her not understanding the gravity of Truin's situation, but deep down he knew better.

An hour before dawn, rifle shots, then an explosion shook the old structure, waking everyone. Charlie jumped up and ran to the door. Flairs lit up the sky in front of the berm walls.

"Charlie?" Vouc said.

"Stay here," he ordered, and ran into the main room just as Khanh dived through the open door. "Bob! You ok?" he called from across the room.

"Ok."

Rifles all along the berm opened up. Another explosion above them and the tower was quickly set ablaze. Illumination continued to light up the sky, but Charlie still could not see what happened to the guards posted there.

The barracks emptied. Everyone ran to the berm. The machine gun positioned directly in front of them began firing. He saw the American sergeant running along the berm wall shouting orders in English.

Under attack from whom? Charlie was confused. Then he remembered the boy with the message who ran into the jungle. "Hey Sarge," he called to the staff sergeant. "Who is it?"

"Damned if I know," came the reply. "Could be Cao Dai or Viet Minh."

Bullets peppered the wall of their building. He saw several of the village men run past him. They were not carrying their weapons, which greatly concerned Charlie. "Give me a weapon," he called.

Ramirez slid a .45 across the floor. "Out here, I carry an extra," he said. The soldier, prone on the floor, looked through the partially open door for a target. Charlie crawled to a window. They heard explosions near the gate, and began to fire in that direction. Two villagers fell from the berm and lay in the red mud.

"Get ready for an assault," Ramirez called. Without a weapon, Bob braced himself against the wall. "Like in Korea," the staff sergeant said.

They both opened up as men clad in military fatigues rushed through the opened gate. Several took cover while the remainder ran the berm to surround the house. Charlie quickly counted eight or nine men.

Ramirez's sergeant rolled through the door and crawled to the staff sergeant. "We're it, Sarge," he announced. Our boys are either knocked out of action or they ran."

Firing from outside the command shack diminished, then ended.

"American, no hurt. Want Madame Thieu," someone yelled from behind Bob's car. Charlie was impressed with their fire discipline. *Combat tested,* he thought.

Vouc entered the room and scurried over to Charlie. "Viet Minh. I know," she whispered to Charlie.

"Sarge, what do you want to do?" he asked.

Ramirez gave him a blank look. "Hell, I don't know, but the woman is damned popular, ain't she?"

"Yup."

"Since it's just the five of us, we talk." Ramirez pulled out a white handkerchief. He waved it out the window. "Parley! Parley!" he called out.

"Out, out," the man replied. "We talk."

"I'll go, Sarge, and Bob can come with me to translate."

"My command, Stanek. I'll go. Bob?"

Vouc and Khanh spoke rapidly to each other in Vietnamese.

"No Sergeant, I will go," Vouc said.

"Let's go then," Ramirez said.

"No," Charlie protested, but neither changed their mind.

Waving the handkerchief over his head, the two moved slowly out into the yard. When they neared Bob's vehicle, the two men behind it walked around to join them. A cloud of suspicion hung in the air, like two alien worlds trying to avoid collision.

Ramirez spoke and Vouc translated. The leader spoke in return to the American and again, Vouc translated. Finally, Charlie clearly heard her soft voice, as she seemed to speak at great length to the leader.

He seemed to understand that Madame Thieu was no longer in the compound, but insisted that he and the other man conduct a search. Following Vouc's translation, Ramirez agreed.

They entered the building and Ramirez led the two through each room. Vouc followed. Charlie, Bob, and the American soldier stayed near the door. They still held their weapons. Finishing their inspection, the two returned to the main room.

"Americans no problem," the leader said, looking at Ramirez in his U.S. Army fatigues. Charlie saw that he was a young man and appeared very confident. *Probably after spending his youth fighting the French,* he decided.

"He say Truin is friend. Told she was in grave danger, and ordered to rescue her. Diem break agreement. No good," Vouc translated.

"What agreement?" Charlie asked.

Vouc looked at him. "Until elections, people who desire can go north and those in the north can come south without trouble. Everyone agree. Now..." She shrugged.

The leader spoke again. "Why men in tower shoot at us. We not French." Vouc translated.

The Americans had no answer.

The three decided to take a chance on the road south. Bob thought it was in better shape after the rains, but he was mistaken. They spent most of the trip fighting mud and deep, water-filled potholes. They arrived in Saigon and the hotel in the darkness. After spending much of the journey pushing the old Citroen out of the mud, Charlie was exhausted. But he knew he had to speak with Jack.

The bastard was holding back, he thought. *I knew there was something he would not tell me.* He escorted Vouc to her suite and returned to his floor. He immediately knocked on Jack's door. Too exhausted to be angry, he decided to confront him directly but rationally.

The door opened after the fourth or fifth knock. Jack stood in front of him partially dressed. They stared at each other, as if one was trying to read the other's mind.

Charlie could not hold back. He threw a punch that landed across Jack's jaw, knocking the former fighter back against a chair.

"You lying bastard," Charlie hissed. He stood over Jack. "Talk to me."

"Now you want to talk," he replied, rubbing his jaw. Slowly, he raised himself up to the chair. "That's a great right you have. Sure you never boxed?"

"You have her, don't you?"

"Not really, buddy."

"Don't call me 'buddy.'" Charlie was slowly calming down. "Talk, damn it!"

"Ok, ok. Sit down." He waited for Charlie to sit. "Barton and another guy named West with some Vietnamese soldiers picked her up couple of days ago. I wasn't along with them."

"But you knew about it. When we talked you knew she had been captured."

"We got the message from Ramirez when we were in DaLat. The general was with us, standing beside Barton. He insisted his men accompany Barton. I stayed in DaLat. I had other work to do."

"Where is Barton holding her? Tell me," Charlie demanded.

Jack sighed. "We don't have her."

"What? Liar."

"That's the truth, Charlie," Jack replied, looking away. "When they returned to DaLat, the general insisted they take custody of her. Just the three of us and a room full of Vietnamese soldiers. What could we do?"

"You gave her up. Just like that, you gave her up," Charlie said softly, He placed his head in his hands. "Why do they want her so badly?" he whispered.

"The Army wants to know where Le Doan is. He's leading the commies here in the south, and they figure they get him and they get the whole show here in South Vietnam sewed up."

"What do they expect to learn from Madame Thieu?"

Jack stared at him. "Hey, I don't think you realize how powerful...and influential your lover is."

"What are you saying?"

"The general said she knows everything about the Viet Minh infrastructure in the south," Jack said.

"Then she should be sent north as per agreements between the North and the South."

"Maybe she will be...if they don't torture her to death. Sorry, but that's the way it is, so pack your bag and let's get the hell out of here. My work is almost completed."

"You keep saying that." Charlie stood. "You go. I'm staying until her situation is resolved. "I'll get her to safety, or..." He walked to the door.

"Or?" Jack asked, but not surprised by Charlie's iron determination. He knew it was his MO, said so in the dossier. "What if they kill her? Hell, what if she's already dead?" Jack said it softly to Charlie's back.

"If they kill her, I will hold the general or Barton personally responsible." Charlie said it loud enough so Jack was sure to hear. His threat was undeniable.

"What does that mean?"

"Get out of the country, Jack. My war's just begun."

"Shit." Jack suddenly understood that this guy is very serious and that frightened him. "You don't fool around, do you?"

"No!"

"Watch your step, buddy, and stay away from me and my mission. If you don't, it will mean real trouble for you."

"That sounds like a threat," Charlie hissed from across the room.

The door slammed shut and he was gone.

Chapter 12

"In Ngo Dinh Diem, South Vietnam has found a strong democratic leader to stop the Communists," read the headline of the *Los Angeles Times* on May 16. Vouc showed him the paper the following morning. *Who has Betty been interviewing?* Charlie wondered. *Probably a wire service feed.* He did not see her byline.

Vouc watched him while he quickly thumbed through the newspaper.

He felt her eyes on him. "What now?" he asked.

"Mr. Jack leave early before sun," she told him.

"Alone?" Charlie asked.

"Another American pick him up. They meet in lobby. I watch."

Charlie was thinking it might be time to pay Colonel Archer and Barton another visit. "The general has her. Jack confirmed it last night."

"The general's army grows stronger. Khanh tell me this. Prime Minister moves against all who oppose his rule. The

Hoa Hao is next, then Viet Minh who stay in south. That is why Truin never free from him. I worry."

"Yeah? Tonight we talk," he said, turned and made for the door.

"Charlie," Vouc called after him.

He stopped and turned.

"Be careful. General Duc is a dangerous man."

He nodded. Charlie had planned to have Bob take him to Binh Hoa, but decided on a quick detour. *The Frenchman,* he decided walking in the direction of the Intercontinental. He hoped to catch him before he was out for the day.

Charlie found him standing in the lobby when he entered. He walked over to the reporter. "Can I have a moment, Monsieur Chastain?" he asked.

"Of course," Chastain replied politely. "Over here." He led Charlie to chairs in a far corner of the lobby away from prying ears. They sat. "I can tell, Major, that there is a problem, a political problem, and those problems are very complicated.

"That's an understatement," Charlie replied. Sitting on the edge of his chair, he looked the Frenchman in the eyes. "My task is really very simple—to find Madame Thieu and get her out of the country."

He nodded. "Yes, Madame Thieu...Then you have many enemies, Major. Even you Americans want her, but why are you so different from them?" Chastain smiled broadly. "Oh, of course, you are in love with her, yes?"

"She's an old friend in trouble." Charlie said. "From ten years ago when it was the Japanese who controlled this land."

"The deepest kind of love. I am French. I know this."

"I've been working with her niece, and so far, everyone is one step ahead of us."

"Co Vouc?"

"Yes."

"Be careful with that one, Major. Like many here she must play politics to survive," he said, serious. "Did you know she is promised to marry General Duc's son. He still expects her to marry him, even though he hides in Paris.

"What does that mean?" Charlie remembered what she had said about the general—friends, just friends.

"Their families are close."

"I thought she might also have connections to the Viet Minh. Because of Madame Thieu."

"No, she like most of her family were, are aristocrats. It's a very small club," he said. If something should happen to Madame Thieu, Vouc inherits everything. No close relatives other than Vouc's brother who also hides in Paris." He shrugged. That motivates many, eh major?"

"Thanks for the briefing, Monsieur Chastain. I'll remember what you've shared with me."

The Frenchman smiled pleasantly. "One thing to keep in mind, Major."

"What's that?"

"Diem won't kill her...if he has her." Chastain stood and extended his hand. "The others? Well, I do not know, not even about the American intelligence services here. Good luck with your search."

"Thank you. You've been very helpful." Charlie shook his hand.

Both men departed the lobby, Chastain out the doors walking while Charlie found Bob. He got in the Citroen before the Vietnamese opened the door for him.

"Bob, it seems you're the only person in this country I can trust."

"Yes, Major. I tell you straight up. No lie."

"Good to hear that," Charlie replied. "Now, here's the story. General Duc and Diem have Truin."

"No good," Bob said, concerned. He sat behind the wheel motionless.

"How can we free her? You and me."

"Other Americans help us?"

"No."

Bob thought without speaking. "If General Duc still in DaLat, then we must go there," he finally said.

"With all the roadblocks?"

"We must go other way."

"Isn't that road controlled by the Viet Minh?"

"Yes, but no worry. Other son in jungle with them, and we need their help."

"Will they?"

"We talk with commander, Le Doan."

"Can we find him and will he offer assistance?

"Yes."

"Do we take Co Vouc with us?"

"No."

That surprised Charlie. "If we rescue her, what happens then?"

"I think her safe in jungle with Viet Minh."

"You don't think Co Vouc should know about any of this?"

"She too friendly with general."

"What about the Buddhist monk? Can he help us?"

"Don't know. They hate Diem and Viet Minh, but maybe they make own deal, eh?"

"I understand."

Bob turned to look at Charlie. "Major, only people support Madame Thieu. But no one cares what people want. They have no power."

"When do we leave?"

"Now we go," he replied. "We know much about DaLat. You remember?"

"You still have your rifle? We'll need weapons."

"We get from son. They have good guns. They get from Duc Trong. American guns."

"I'm ready."

Chapter 13

Harrison Robinson, a career diplomat, presented his credentials to Prime Minister Diem that same day as the United States' new ambassador to South Vietnam. The Secretary of State has ordered him to give loyal and sincere support to Diem's government. General Stone had flown out to Guam two days prior. For the moment, Colonel Archer commanded all American soldiers in the country.

Unknown to Charlie, the change in American policy toward the Diem government largely rendered his mission unnecessary, and with Madame Thieu in custody, his reason for being in country as an official representative of the U.S. Government void and potentially embarrassing for the Americans.

Charlie and Bob were on the road and moving quickly north to DaLat. The road was passable and they made good time. They were dedicated to rescuing Truin and neither cared much for the current state of U.S., South Vietnamese relations.

Charlie stared out the window, marveling at the changing landscape as they slowly rose in elevation to Bao Loc, then to

Duc Trong. They passed through farming villages with the layered rice paddies surrounding them. Small children rode water buffalo to guide them through their daily chores that included plowing ground for the next planting to turning a wooden wheel to pump water. The scene was bucolic and serene. They saw no soldiers along the drive.

Between Bao Loc and Duc Trang, Bob pulled the car over along the road but under a stand of bamboo. "We hide car, then walk." He pointed out a distant village, secluded in a small stand of trees. Only the rooftops with whiffs of smoke trailing into the deep blue sky were visible. "Come," he said to Charlie.

They walked for about a mile, meeting several farmers along the way. They were friendly but stared at Charlie. Finally, the two entered a cluster of thatched houses. Children ran to greet them.

Charlie saw that the small village nestled in a narrow ravine and up against the rising mountains. The jungle canape thickened dramatically the closer they walked toward the mountains. Charlie followed Bob who seemed to know where he was going.

An older man walked toward them as they entered the central square. They greeted each other with bows and pleasantries, and then Bob spoke at great length to the man. Charlie figured he was providing him who Charlie believed was the Village Chief with an explanation of why they were there and what they wanted from him. He hoped.

The conversation at an end, Bob turned to Charlie. "We go," he said. The Chief prepared to blindfold Charlie but Bob stopped him, speaking rapidly.

The man nodded and stuck the crude cotton cloth in a pocket.

The three departed the village into the ravine, the villager leading the way. They followed a narrow path, barely visible, through thick vegetation. A new world for Charlie. Dense jungle teaming with wildlife. It was a far cry from the desolation of south central Australia. They walked an hour and rounded a curve as they moved higher in elevation.

A young man in fatigues and carrying an American rifle stepped out of the vegetation to block their way. He spoke with the old man. Charlie watched closely, plotting an escape if necessary.

Bob joined their conversation. Finally, the young man nodded. He motioned for them to follow, then turned and began walking. At this point, the old man left them to return to his village.

"We follow," Bob told Charlie.

The three walked another hour, continuing through the dense vegetation. Others dressed and armed similarly to the first soon joined them. Everyone looked at Charlie. *I am a curiosity out here,* he thought. *Like a chimp in a zoo.*

Now deep into the jungle and about a thousand feet higher than when they began, they entered a small clearing. Charlie saw several small thatched houses built around an open area. There were no side panels. Men and women watched from inside.

"We wait here," Bob said.

"Who are we waiting for?" Charlie asked, growing nervous with armed men surrounding him.

"For the commander," Bob replied.

"Does everyone stay here or are their other encampments?'

Bob smiled and pointed down to the ground with a finger. "Many there," he said.

"Tunnels?"

"Many. I see during war with French," Bob replied. "They say please sit." They sat on the ground and others sat across from them. A young woman brought tea.

"Drink," Bob said. "Very polite. Must drink."

They sipped their tea and waited. Charlie did not really know who they waited for, but hoped he was their leader. A young man entered the clearing. Bob looked up to see him and suddenly burst into tears. He stood and the two embraced. They spoke quickly among themselves with the others watching enviously. They seemed to take great pleasure in the reunion. *They are home sick,* Charlie thought.

"My number one son, Quac," Bob told Charlie proudly. They both sat beside Charlie.

"American," his son said to Charlie. "Good."

"I explain to son," Bob said. The two—father and son—began an in-depth conversation that Charlie was unable to follow.

"What did he say?" Charlie asked.

"Madame Thieu important. We must rescue her."

"Good."

"Son also say General not here, but commander here. We talk."

"What does that mean?" he asked, trying not to sound disappointed.

"No worry. Nguyen Quan Tran will send men with us. Must hurry before she moved. He send men for her two days ago in Duc Trong. They meet Americans there. Not you?"

"Bob, tell him we were there also to rescue Madame Thieu."

Bob explained to his son.

Nguyen walked into the clearing and over to the group. Everyone but Charlie bowed deferentially to the man. Charlie guessed him to be about his age. *Probably very experienced,* he thought. Bob's son stepped forward to brief him. They looked to Charlie. The commander seemed to be sizing him up. He motioned Bob over.

They spoke more. Bob returned to sit beside Charlie. "He said not to worry. She die before she talk."

Charlie was not reassured. "Will he help to rescue her?"

"Yes."

"Save her, yes," Quac added. "Prison bad. Must go before they take her to Saigon."

Commander Nguyen produced a crude map and motioned for Bob, Charlie, and Quac with six others to join him. They gathered around the map that Nguyen had posted to the thatched wall of one of the houses.

They spoke, moving fingers on the map, everyone offering something to the conversation. Bob turned to Charlie. "He thinks she is held in hotel. You remember hotel?"

Like an old-fashioned prison break, Charlie thought, still disbelieving he was a part of it. "I remember well the very elegant DaLat Hill Resort, constructed by the French with teak and mahogany," he replied. "The place was surrounded by heavy machine gun emplacements."

"Bob nodded, "Yes."

Charlie in September 1945 represented the U.S. on the Allied Control Commission. He arrived at the DaLat army base, converted from an earlier French outpost and still controlled by the Japanese, who waited patiently before officially surrendering to the Allies.

Truin accompanied me and we had come to take custody of a suspected Japanese war criminal, Captain Suzuki. Yes, Colonel Hamura commanded the base, and they flew Nakajima Dragon Swallowers, a transport plane. He remembered the events clearly.

The commander handed Charlie a pistol, then smiled. "Major Charles Stanek," he said in perfect English. He bowed again.

Charlie looked at it. A Tokarev, he saw. Everyone in the group smiled and nodded to him.

"He say you very famous. The man who escaped the Russian called Pavlov. An honor," Bob translated. "He also say the Russians are worse that the French but they are our friends."

Charlie handled the weapon. It brought back memories of the war and his escape from General Pavlov. "Thank you," he said. "It is my honor to serve with such fine soldiers." Bob translated. "I know this weapon well," Charlie said, smiling at the commander.

Everyone appreciated Charlie's response. Each man nodded and shook his hand.

He was surprised at the details considered in their planning. In addition to weapons, they gathered rope and explosives. The commander decided that Charlie, Bob, and six others would make the trip to Da Lat.

"Not enough," Charlie said. "The army is there."

"No worry," Bob told him. "Most soldiers outside DaLat on roads, not in jungle. We have friends there who work at hotel. The commander send message now that they must help."

They watched a young man depart.

"Commander say you stay outside hotel—hide. They must not know an American with us. Be quiet, no shoot. We grab her and go. He send message also to Madame Thieu to get ready."

Charlie hesitated.

Bob saw the hesitation, but said nothing.

Charlie reconsidered, knowing it made sense for him to stay hidden. He finally agreed.

"Some in Army no like Diem so they no see what we do. You understand?"

Charlie nodded that he understood.

"When dark we go," Bob said. "Maybe three hours to walk. Get there when everyone asleep. Ok?"

And General Duc? Where is he?"

Bob laughed. "General drink too much and go to sleep like Emperor Bao Dai."

Charlie was impressed. *They've done this before,* he decided.

Everyone finished their preparations, and then waited for darkness. Charlie lay on the ground and gazed up at a sky filled with stars, his Tokarev neatly tucked into his belt. The sky reminded him of Australia and made him homesick, too.

He had given up on making a plan, deciding to let things happen, a policy he was doing often it now seemed. *Hell. I have no control over events, anyway. If we can get Truin to safety, I will get back to Saigon and fly home,* he thought. *I have done all I can here.*

As clouds suddenly began to form and cover the stars, they departed. The night turned even darker. They followed a narrow path, going north, Charlie decided, looking at the rapidly disappearing stars. They walked single file, close together with Charlie in the middle.

Except for an occasional bird squawking, silence surrounded them. He looked up at the clouds quickly covering the moon. In complete darkness, he saw only the man in front of him.

He was impressed with how quiet their movement was. He heard not a cough or jungle of equipment. *Real discipline,* he thought, feeling more reassured. *They know what they are doing.*

Not accustomed to the rough, rocky terrain, he stumbled in the dark several times, but otherwise, he kept up to the rapid pace, breathing heavily. It had been awhile.

Chapter 14

A sudden downpour drenched them as they made their way out of the jungle onto the plateau. DaLat was close. He felt it in is bones. Leaving the jungle canape, the team spread out, spaced out with more than ten meters between them.

"Soon," Bob whispered from behind Charlie.

Charlie was drenched first in perspiration, and then soaked with rain as the cloud opened up on them. They stopped hourly to reorganize and take a sip of water. He saw not another human in the three-hour trek.

Soon, Charlie looked up and saw the hotel looming before him like some giant living behemoth in the fog and drizzle. Without a word spoken, each man moved to his designated position.

They stealthily moved through the tall grass avoiding the guard outposts. Finally, they stood facing the three-story window where they believed Madame Thieu held. From his position, Charlie looked up at a window. *A light visible through the glass, indicating the room was occupied, hopefully by Truin,* Charlie thought.

Before they moved closer, he saw a sentry in the shadows. *Have to take him out,* Charlie decided. He hoped someone in front overpowered him and killed him, if necessary.

He heard a short whistling sound, and the sentry stopped.

Shit, Charlie thought, *discovered,* but the sentry returned the sound, and then kneeled near the tall grass. Two men moved forward and spoke briefly with the soldier. The three entered the hotel.

They waited with growing impatience. Bob lay in the tall elephant grass next to Charlie. The minutes ticked away. The lighted window on the third floor opened. A knotted hemp rope fell to the ground from the window.

Good, good, Charlie thought, watching.

A man stepped out on the ledge and scurried down the rope, one knot at a time. Then another figure stepped on out on the ledge, slowly and awkwardly managing the rope.

"Madame Thieu," Bob whispered, excited. "I get her." He stood and quickly ran through the grass to position himself under the window. Charlie stood and followed at a safe distance to the edge of the tall grass.

Suddenly, they heard yelling from inside the hotel. Lights came on, first on the top floor, then cascading down to the first floor.

Charlie left the cover of the tall grass to move closer to the building to support Bob and the other men assisting Truin. He had drawn his pistol and prepared to fire.

Truin jumped the last few feet to the ground with the last man just over her, who did the same. Now everyone was on the ground and running into the tall grass.

Soldiers stood at the window yelling. They began to fire with rifles. Charlie and the others held their fire until everyone was deep in the grass, then opened up on the window.

Sentries from the other side of the building came around to support those at the doorway. Other soldiers pushed through the doorway to take cover across the lawns. They fired into the tall grass

"Charlie," Truin said, surprised. She seemed very happy to see him. She hugged him

"Go," Charlie ordered, and Truin with Bob ran further into the grass, making for the tree line. He opened up with the Tokarev. The three men beside him fired rifles to cover their escape.

The soldiers returned fire, some standing while others shot from the ground. Firing from the window also continued with bullets zipping through the tall grass

Time to go, Charlie decided. He turned to follow Truin and Bob deeper into the tall grass.

The soldiers stood to advance on them while the Viet Minh continued their volley of small arms fire. Charlie heard bullets zinging over his head and lower, nipping at the blades of grass around him. The soldiers had found a larger target and Charlie realized he may have been identified.

The last of the team pulled back, to disappear into the grass. Charlie reached the tree line beyond the soldiers' view, to Bob and Truin. He saw the commander forming some type of defensive line with his men just inside the trees.

"Didi," someone yelled. Truin, Bob, and Charlie sprinted for the deep forest. Behind them, firing intensified as the remainder of the team fired as one at the National Army soldiers.

Charlie never looked back. They headed toward a rendezvous spot designated earlier. Finally reaching it, all three collapsed to the ground. Lying against a tree, Charlie pulled out the pistol and checked its magazine. Empty. He began to reload from his pocket. Luckily, the commander had provided him with extra ammo.

Slowly, two at a time, the men trickled into the site. But Charlie still heard gunfire. When everyone had returned unharmed, the commander gave orders to his men. They began to move out single-file, with Charlie and Truin in the middle. Within a short distance, they veered off onto a different trail. The patrol leader left two men behind to cover their retreat.

About half way back, they stopped for a break. They wanted to allow the two men left behind to catch up. Truin sat beside Charlie.

"I knew you would come for me," she said and kissed him on the cheek.

"I had to," he said, holding her hand. "I couldn't leave until I knew you were safe."

She smiled. "Tomorrow, they take me to Binh Hoa, to a place General Duc say the Americans will talk to me. His idea. He say there Americans will learn where Le Doan hide. They have special methods. I very frightened." She kissed him again on the cheek. This was a thank you kiss.

Charlie was relieved. *We acted just in time,* he thought. "You must thank Khanh. If it wasn't for his knowledge and contacts I would have failed."

"Yes, "she said, "we are comrades."

Bob, hearing the conversation, smiled.

The sky was clearing and the moon low in the sky guided their way back. They arrived at the base camp in the early dawn hours exhausted. Each took off their gear, stacked their weapons and collapsed to the ground.

The two left behind finally joined them, and immediately told their story to the group. Everyone sipped their tea and listened. "Soldiers follow them into the jungle, but few. They shoot and we lead them down wrong trail. Soldiers follow but soon give up search and return to DaLat. We stay on old trail."

When they finished, everyone cheered and patted the team members on the back. "It was a story of success. Another victory," everyone agreed.

Bob sat beside Charlie to translate. Truin sat in front of Charlie, enjoying his warmth and strength, but also adding flavor to Bob's retelling.

"They're brave men," Charlie said when he completed the story.

"Yes, but soldiers afraid, too," Bob corrected him with a smile.

Charlie knew he had to return to Saigon before Jack missed him, but he was not ready to say goodbye to Truin. Seeing her again only reinforced his feelings for her. He watched her move about the camp, talking with men and women. She was important, he saw.

"Bob," Charlie said later that day. "Take the money and go." He handed Bob piaster and American dollars—all he had.

Bob took the money. "Enough," he said, after counting it.

"Return in five days. I'll meet you where we hid the car."

The next few days Truin and he spent together were peaceful and uneventful. Charlie was surprised to learn that in Le Doan's absence, Truin was in command. Regardless of her duties, the two spent their time together well, mostly talking, and holding hands when no one watched. The others recognized their bond and went out of their way to give them time alone.

She understood that she could not return to Saigon and the Dragon House without arrest. She accepted that.

"What will you do now?" Charlie asked. He did not really know what to expect in reply.

"I will stay here and wait for the elections," she said. "These are my people."

"Charlie understood.

"Will you stay in Vietnam or go to your home?"

Charlie sighed deeply. "I have been here almost two months. I have a son and a ranch I must return to." There was sadness in his voice.

Truin held his hand tightly. "I understand," she said. "Soon, when we have peace again and democracy, we will meet again, my love." She rested her head on his shoulders.

Bob was waiting when Charlie reached their meeting place. Truin had accompanied him as far as the village. They embraced one last time, and then said their farewells.

"Saigon," Bob said with a smile. "We talk in car."

Charlie sat up front with Bob. They were silent until they passed again through Bao Loc, then Bob spoke. "General Duc angry. He blame soldiers for escape, but he know she gone."

"Hopefully, he'll stop searching for her."

"Never," Bob replied. "Soldiers around hotel. Day and night, they watch."

Charlie shook his head.

When they arrived at Dragon House, Charlie entered and walked directly to the elevator. Before he reached it, he heard his name called. "Charlie. Charlie." He turned to see Co Vouc standing behind him in the lobby.

"Co Vouc?"

"Where you go?" she asked, demanding an answer.

"The country. I wanted to see more of it before returning to Australia," he lied. *He knew she was disbelieving, but so what.*

"How you go without me?" she asked, a hint of anger in her voice.

"Khanh," he replied.

"Why you not tell me?" she demanded to know. "We work together, yes?"

She's angry, Charlie decided. "You were too busy with hotel." He then saw the soldiers. They seemed to surround the place...and him. They watched.

"Other American look for you," Vouc said. "Every day you gone."

"Jack? Where is he now?"

"May be upstairs," she said. "He ask about you and I say I don't know." She kept her distance. "Tonight we talk...in my room."

"I'll find Jack." He entered the elevator, the door closed on the conversation. Up he went.

He knocked hard on Jack's door, not knowing if he would find him in the room.

The door opened immediately. "Charlie," Jack said, surprised. "Where the hell you been?"

"Out in the country, mostly," Charlie replied. "I've been looking for Madame Thieu, but I've failed to find her."

"Yeah? Come in." He held the door wide and Charlie entered to sit in the nearest chair. Jack sat beside him. "We need to talk." Jack sounded formal, as if he were about to be interrogated. Charlie knew the training.

"Got anything to drink?"

"Beer."

"That works...in a glass."

Jack stood and walked to a table, got two beers and a glass. He opened both. "It's warm," he said, pouring one into the glass. He handed Charlie the glass of beer. Jack's bottle foamed over around the edge, but he took a swallow anyway.

"I want to hear all about your travels," he said, sitting down again. "Let me see...You've been gone about a week."

Charlie told a story of travel to Vung Tao and up the coast to Nha Trang, walking on white sand beaches, sleeping in primitive surroundings. He knew Jack would never believe him, but also knew he could not prove otherwise.

Jack quietly sipped the warm beer and listened. "Lots happened in your absence," he said when Charlie had finished.

Charlie ignored the statement. "Well, if your work here is completed, we can return to Australia. I guess I'm finally ready to leave."

"So, all of a sudden you're ready to go. What has changed your mind?"

"Nothing more I can do here with the change in mission and the disappearance of Madame Thieu," he said. "Anyway, I got a kid I must return to. When do we leave?"

Jack stared at him. "You're ready to leave," he mumbled. "Colonel Archer wants to meet with you...now."

"Tomorrow. I need to relax, put my feet up," Charlie said. "He can wait. I'm not his lapdog."

"Now means now. We go," Jack said with growing anger and frustration. "Get up."

They got in a Jeep parked next to the hotel. Jack drove. "I see you're moving up here, Jack," Charlie commented. "Got your own transportation."

"Yup."

"What have you been doing the last week?" Charlie asked, as they passed through the city on their way to Binh Hoa.

"I was in Binh Hoa...and DaLat."

"Why DaLat?" he asked, wanting to hear his reply.

"We'll talk about that later."

"Did you finally get your hands on Madame Thieu?"

"Fuck you," Jack growled, missed a gear, and the transmission ground. Passers-by looked curiously at the two foreigners.

For the first time, Charlie noticed the beauty of the countryside. People moved along the road, some with bundles on their backs and others with carts, walking back and forth from the city. The vegetation was lush. Flowers were blooming, all much different from central Australia with its rugged dryness. To Charlie, everything seemed so peaceful, not angry and divided. *It will never last,* he decided cynically.

Nearing Bien Hoa, they met a growing number of Vietnamese soldiers, most walking along the highway, rifles slung. *Diem's army is growing and that translates into more power for him,* he decided as two American Sherman tanks rumbled by.

Chapter 15

Are you trying to start your own little war here, Stanek? Colonel Archer asked, his anger exploding. He nervously paced about his office but never taking his eyes off Charlie. In the room were Charlie, Jack, and Barton, in addition to Archer. While Archer stood, the others sat in a semi-circle around his desk. "General Duc is beside himself with anger. He believed the taller man his soldiers saw was Russian or Chinese, I had to set him straight."

"What's the proof I was somehow involve..." Charlie tried to say.

"Shut up, Major," Archer interrupted.

"We had her," Barton jumped in uninvited. "We should have locked her tighter with more guards, but the general said it was not necessary."

"Yeah, yeah, excuses," Archer growled. "Now we'll never get her."

"Why is she so damn important to you," Charlie asked, but knowing the answer.

Archer stopped pacing. He sighed long and hard. "Listen, Diem is our man. The Viet Minh are organizing in the south and they must be stopped." He sat down, lit an American cigarette, and exhaled slowly trying to calm himself. "The Commies are a formidable force that can block Diem's consolidation of power. Stability means ridding the South of the Viet Minh, whatever that takes. And you...you damn it, helped her escape." He pointed his finger at Charlie.

"I don't know anything about it, and I don't know anything about the Viet Minh or their leaders. You're the fucking expert here, Colonel. Tell us the plan. You got one? While you're at it, tell us the plan for this paramilitary force you're building."

"Fuck you!"

"The Viet Minh are going north during the exchange, aren't they?" Jack asked. "They'll take her with them.

Charlie and Colonel Archer turned to stare at him.

"Hell no! They're organizing to stay, damn it," Archer screamed at him. "Don't you read any of the intelligence reports we're getting? Jesus," he said, lighting another cigarette from the butt of the earlier.

"They think they are going to win next year," Barton added.

"What about our efforts in the villages building local forces?" Charlie asked, curious to a response.

"Answer him, Barton," Archer ordered.

"That will take several years, and we don't have several years if the elections are in '56," he answered.

"If they're operating out of the jungle, why not get the general to attack them? Surely he has the manpower and the hardware," Jack asked innocently.

"General Duc says he's not ready," Archer said.

"He'll never be ready," Charlie felt he had to say. "He's too busy drinking and whoring, I hear. I figure it'll take the U.S. Marines to flush them out." He tried to mask his sarcasm but failed miserably.

"We're training them, arming them. They'll be ready sooner than you think." Barton tried to be positive. "But we need more men to train them."

"Just let things take their natural course, Colonel. Even the Viet Minh don't dislike Americans."

"How the hell do you know that, major?"

"The talk around town." He smiled.

They were silent, choosing to stare at Charlie instead.

"You think you know everything, don't you? But you don't." Archer finally broke the silence, visibly exasperated. "I got Washington breathing down my neck, and now with the new ambassador that came on station..." He walked around the desk to stand in front of Charlie. "Are you part of the team or not?" He waited as the others did, for his answer.

"I'm going home to take care of my son and herd sheep, Colonel," he said slowly so everyone knew exactly where he was coming from. "This is your fucking mess not mine."

"We'll see about that, Major." Archer stressed the last word.

"I've had enough of this. Good day, gentlemen." Charlie stood and prepared to leave.

"Consider yourself under house arrest, Major. General Duc insists and now I think it's a good idea. I'm ordering you not to leave the hotel."

"You can't do that. I am an American citizen in a sovereign nation. You don't have that authority."

"Try me," Archer said bitterly. "When you decide to be more cooperative and forthcoming, let me know."

The return trip to Saigon was quiet. Jack drove and Charlie sat beside him brooding.

"The National Army is guarding the hotel 24/7, Charlie. How you going to handle that?"

Charlie looked at him with contempt. "How am I supposed to handle it, Jack? Escape into the jungle?" He paused. "Hell,

I may try that route. Cambodia is close and the Viet Minh are even closer."

"If you have information on the woman and how to locate her, tell them, then we can get the hell out of here."

"Jack, as far as I can see, you can leave anytime," he replied. "Your work is finished. Just jump a hop out."

"Right now, you're my work," Jack said. "And I think you need me to keep the general off your back."

"How are you going to do that?"

"Duc knows me and I think will listen to me."

"Right."

Jack parked the Jeep close to the hotel and both men entered the lobby. "Hungry?" Jack asked.

"What else do I have to do?" Charlie growled.

Co Vouc silently watched them walk through the lobby. Neither man looked at her, choosing to navigate politely around the soldiers congregating there. "Bastards," Charlie said under his breath. They walked toward the small restaurant the Dragon House offered its guests.

Charlie continued brooding, ordered fruit and tea, and stared out the window, at the armed guards outside. He did not speak.

"You're one solitary son of a bitch. Yup, all alone in the world," Jack finally said. "And you like it that way, don't you?" A young man served them and they began eating.

"If you try to escape, I'll follow you."

Charlie sensed he was not kidding.

The soldiers watched them while they ate.

Bastards are guarding me like a serial killer, Charlie thought, and turned to look at Jack. "Better keep an eye on me then."

"If you plan to make the Agency your career, you will be just like me...or dead. Remember that. A small player in their scheme of things."

Jack was not listening. "You're my responsibility now, according to Archer. Where you go I go."

"That your mission here? Watching me," Charlie said. "But I think there's something more to your mission, Jack, and I'll figure it out."

"Jack said nothing.

Charlie stood to leave. "There's trouble ahead, Jack, and if you don't leave now, it'll hit you head on. I think you're more deeply involved than you let on. Watch your step. The Vietnamese aren't stupid. Hell, they're probably watching you right now." He sighed, feeling frustrated. "See you later."

"What? Stop! Tell me what that means."

Charlie kept walking. *He's no different from the others, thinking they can shape these people the way they want them. They are using me anyway they can to accomplish that.*

Back in his room, he lay on the bed, trying to think things through. *Hell, they could keep me prisoner here for a couple of days or months even, if I don't tell them what they want to know.* He thought about Hao Lung Prison, and the dungeon in Prague where Pavlov held him, tortured him.

A knock at the door.

"Come in, damn it," he called, thinking it was Jack.

The door opened and Co Vouc walked in.

"Vouc," Charlie said, surprised.

"Charlie, we must talk. She was dressed casually in Western clothes. She had let her dark hair down. She walked to the bed and sat on the edge beside Charlie. "I miss you," she said.

"Yeah?" he replied. "Sorry we didn't tell you about the trip, but I was rushed."

"Soldiers tell me that Truin escape. Did you help?"

"I guess everyone is talking about that, but no, I was in Vung Tau."

She smiled. "You lie, but ok. Truin is safe now."

"Good to hear," Charlie replied. "She escaped from your father in law."

Vouc paused, surprised by the statement. "Khanh tell you. I know."

"You've kept many secrets from me, Vouc."

"Charlie, is family politics," she replied, diverting eye contact. "But I never want to hurt you." She touched his arm. "Please, always remember: In Vietnam, no one hurt you."

He wondered what she meant but said nothing. "Will you be married here in Saigon or Paris?" he finally asked. "They say Paris is lovely this time of year."

"No, never marry him," she said angrily. "He lazy coward. Never."

"I'll bet the general doesn't know how you feel about his son."

"Me a woman. My feelings are not important."

What is she saying? Charlie wondered. "You play politics with the general, yes?"

"My feelings are for you. Truin is gone and I fear you never see again."

"What do you want from me, Vouc? I'm a prisoner here. I can't even leave the hotel."

"I want you to stay." She touched his hand, and then bent to kiss it. "I'm a woman, too."

"A very beautiful woman," he replied. Charlie was curious as to her motive here.

"I show you." She stood and slowly disrobed. Shedding everything, she stood proudly naked before him. "You see. I like Truin."

"I see."

"Please touch me, Charlie." She slid into his bed, moving close to him. Her small breasts touched him. She placed his hands on them. "All over...please. I love you."

"What do I do now? he wondered, not wanting this to happen. *However, if I refuse her, then what? She may be my only ticket out of here.* He kissed her on the lips, but he saw that was not enough. He messaged her body, soft and so white. Unable to resist her, he rubbed her thighs slowly, delicately using his fingers.

She moaned softly in his ear.

He continued with his hands. Vouc reached lower to his trousers, deftly unbuttoning them. She held him with her hand, pulling him as she rolled onto her back.

"Like a woman, Charlie."

She's been here before, he decided but having no interest at the moment in discussing lovers with her. He moved to cover her smaller body with his own.

They lay together, neither speaking. Then, Vouc kissed him on the cheek, rolled out of bed, grabbed her clothing, and entered the bath. She returned fully dressed and kissed him again. "I go," she said. "Work now. Tomorrow."

Their evening trysts continued for several more days. *The woman is insatiable,* Charlie thought. He was exhausted. Much as he did every day since his arrest, he lay in bed considering his dilemma. *At least, they didn't take my U.S. passport, so clean and new with the Republic of South Vietnam stamp. He smiled. And I'm still a Major in the U.S. Army on special assignment. It should be valid anywhere I go, as long as I don't travel to China or the U.S.S.R.*

Jack was wrong, he decided. *I am not a loner. I got a son I must get back to, and a thousand head of sheep to sheer. But traveling alone was better. He had learned that trying to escape from Czechoslovakia.*

I will probably never see Truin again, but she's safe for the moment anyway, and out of reach of General Duc and the Americans. What made Charlie the angriest and very frustrated *was not that they expected me to pump information from her, but that I share their ideological views for Indochina—stopping the Chinese from overrunning all Southeast Asia. Colonel Archer sees the Vietnamese, people like Khanh and Vouc, as only means to an end. Do they really believe they can give the Vietnamese guns, airplanes, and training to fight their proxy war, and then just pick up and go home? Mission accomplished. Fool. I refuse to be a part of any of that. So, I have made my decision. Now, how do I get out of here?* The latter began to consume his thoughts.

Early evening came a knock on Charlie's door. He was expecting Vouc, but opening the door, he was surprised to see Jack.

"Wasn't expecting you," he said, but allowed him entrance. "What have you been doing?"

"My job," Jack replied curtly.

"Which is?"

Jack entered and sat down. He gave Charlie a hard look. "Now it's you, like I told you before."

"You going to torture me?" Charlie thought his comment was amusing but Jack did not share that opinion.

"Archer wants me to give it another try," he said. "He wants information on the location of the Viet Minh command structure here in the south."

Charlie sighed. "I can only tell you what I said three days ago. Don't know nothing."

"He said if you don't give us something tangible to go on like a name, coordinates, fuck, anything, you can sit and rot here."

"Come on Jack, help me out here. Get us back to Australia," Charlie pleaded. "I know you have some clout with Archer and Barton."

"Charlie, what is it you called me a couple weeks ago? Oh yeah, a lapdog."

"Hey, I'll give you a job out on my sheep station."

"Thanks for your very generous offer but I decline." He stood. "Get ready for a very long stay at the Dragon House."

"I'm preparing for just that." He knew a threat when he heard it.

Jack opened the door. Two National Army soldiers stood there. "Oh, almost forgot, the officer in charge here is reducing your guards. Thinks you're weakening, I guess."

"Thanks."

"I don't know why I told you that," he said. "Forget I ever mentioned it."

"I will," Charlie replied. *Good information,* he thought, watching the CIA Agent return to his room. *I wonder why he told me that.*

After he saw Jack return to his room, Charlie left to take the elevator down to the lobby. "I have a message," he said to the clerk. Vouc was not around. "Can you get the taxi driver? The one named Khanh. Please ask him to come."

The clerk hesitated, and then called the officer of the guard over. They talked.

"He say ok, but you cannot leave."

"I understand. Khanh. He knows the person to whom I want to deliver the message. She is an American, and I want her to visit. A friend, not Viet Minh. Tell him."

"He told the officer and he agreed, sending a man to find Khanh. Bob returned with the soldier. Seeing Charlie standing there, he smiled. He walked over, bowed and shook Charlie's hand.

"Bob, everything ok?" he asked.

"Yes, no problems," he replied. The soldiers watched.

"They know nothing about me," he whispered.

"Bob, I need you to bring Betty with the American newspaper. You remember?"

"Yes, in Intercontinental. I remember," he said. "Tall and pretty." He motioned with his hands.

"And tell her to bring the latest *Los Angeles Times* along."

"I go."

An hour later, Bob returned with Betty in tow. Charlie was waiting in the lobby. The guards searched her, took the newspaper. They did not unfold it. They then quickly searched her bag. Finding nothing, they allowed her to speak with Charlie.

"Major Charles Stanek, looks like you're in trouble," she said it with a smile and a look of curiosity.

"Just a simple misunderstanding."

"A rogue operator here, I understand."

"You want my story? It might make good reading for the folks back home."

"Home? Which one—Australia or the U.S.?"

"The good old U.S.A.," he replied. "An exclusive on an old spy trapped in Saigon by the U.S. Government."

"I'm ready," she replied, sitting down. "Will they censure it?"

"Nothing top secret. Just my life story."

"Leading to your present predicament?"

"Of course."

"Might make a good read."

"Tomorrow morning here," he said. "I want only one thing from you."

"This is the tough part," she replied. "What?" She looked at him, her eye brows furled.

"I'm stuck here with nothing to do and hell, I don't really know where I'm at," he began. "I would like a map of Indochina."

"I hope I'm not a part of your story. You know...The last part where we die in a daring shoot out."

"Nothing like that," he said. Just some reading along with your newspaper, of course."

She paused to consider the request. "Ok, tomorrow morning, say 8:00."

"Perfect."

The next morning, Charlie came downstairs to find Vouc behind the desk. They spoke briefly and Charlie told her a reporter from the *Los Angeles Times* wanted to interview him. He asked about Jack and she told him he had already left the hotel alone.

Good, he thought, expecting that reply. He could have created unnecessary problems during the interview.

Betty suddenly appeared in the lobby and immediately approached by two soldiers. They searched her, but Betty was prepared, submitting easily. They did not examine the newspaper she carried closely.

Charlie greeted her with a smile. "Let's talk in the dining room, fewer ears, and they will not allow you to come up to my room."

"I'm disappointed," she replied. "I was prepared for more of an intimate interview."

They sat next to a window with a good view of the street. No guards were near them. Sipping tea, Charlie told his story, leaving out many details, especially the salacious ones. He spoke of his service high in the Carpathian Mountains rescuing downed flyers, his mission to Indochina, capture by the Russian General Pavlov and his harrowing escape, his return to Czechoslovakia to rescue a woman and child, and again capture by Russian intelligence. He carefully omitted the killing of the double agent Attila in Bavaria. He explained that the CIA recently approached him to go to Saigon. They wanted him to negotiate with Madame Thieu about a change in government, but unbeknownst to him, they expected him to spy on her for information on the Viet Minh leader.

"I'm now held under house arrest because I could give them no information," he said. "Not believing me, they hold me here."

She asked few questions, writing everything down as Charlie related it. "That's quite a story, Major. I think our readers are particularly interested in your role here and current predicament."

"Oh, don't forget to tell them that I'm just a sheep herder without a mission, who wants only to go home."

"Right." Betty smiled.

"I am hoping that public opinion will force the U.S. Army to release me and allow me to return to my home, but I'm not hopeful," he said. "Listen, I'm not a hero but I do deserve better treatment than I'm getting."

"Oh, I almost forgot. Here is the paper with the requested item." She handed it to him.

"Thanks," he said, taking it in hand.

"Anything else I can get for you to make your stay more comfortable?"

"How about a .45? Can you manage that?"

"That's what I love about you, Major. Your humor."

He shrugged and forced a smile. "Shooting my way out of here is a last resort, anyway."

They stood.

I'll write this up, bring it over and let you have a look, then send it by wire," she said. "Take care, Major. We'll be talking."

Charlie saw Vouc watching them as he escorted Betty through the lobby. He walked over to her, still standing behind the desk. He carefully observed where the captain had positioned his guards.

"Have you spoken with General Duc yet about releasing me?"

"Charlie, you safe here with me," she replied, touching is hand.

He noticed immediately how she touched him—so no one would notice. "I guess that's a 'no.'"

"Aren't you happy here?"

"That's not the issue, Vouc," he replied. "I'm a prisoner."

She sighed and looked away.

"Just a walk around the grounds. Can you arrange that with the Captain of the Guard?"

"I talk with him tonight."

"Thank you," he said. "Don't tell Jack. He would prevent it."

"Ok."

"By the way, has he returned? I have a message I want to leave him. Top Secret. Not in his box."

Vouc paused to think. "Girl who clean room. She let you in."

"Give me ten minutes to get it," he replied. "I'll wait in front of his door." Charlie turned and departed for his room.

He quickly scribbled a note. *Viet Minh to return to DaLat in one day,* he wrote. *Talk later. That should interest him,* he thought, folding the note and walking to the hall. The housekeeper was waiting outside Jack's door. No guards present. She saw him, unlocked the door, and motioned for him to enter.

Charlie smiled, holding up the message for her to see. The woman stood in the doorway, and waited. He walked slowly across the room, scanning as he walked. He did not know exactly what he was looking for, but suspected Jack of being much more than his aide on this trip.

He noticed something in the trash—a crumbled, partially torn piece of correspondence.

The woman continued to wait patiently.

"You clean here?" he asked, motioning at the unmade bed.

She looked at him, and then shook her head.

I have to distract her, he thought. "Who come?" he called, pointing in the hall.

She looked and Charlie immediately grabbed the torn pieces and stuffed them in his pocket. "American?" he asked.

"No," she replied.

Charlie set the message on the bedside table and turned to the woman. "Clean now," he said. "I watch. Very secret," he tried to explain, pointing to the folded slip of paper. He stood in the doorway.

She moved a cart into the room and began to work, mostly replacing towels and making the bed. He pointed to the trash basket. "Take," he said, and she emptied it.

Back in his room, Charlie painstakingly put the pieces of the 'who is Jack Stover' puzzle together. He learned the torn document was a bureaucratic memorandum sent to John Sawyer from a personnel officer in Los Angeles, regarding his pay. *Jack not his real name,* he saw. *He was receiving pay for learning Mandarin Chinese as a second language.* Nevertheless, Charlie found the most interesting bit of information was that Jack had spent most of the last two years working out of the American Embassy in Taiwan, according to the mostly pay-related correspondence. *Therefore, he had not spent any time in Vietnam. Liars.*

He smiled. *You're sloppy, Jack or John.* Charlie set the memo aside and considered. *But why lie to me? What is so secret about his mission that he could not tell me? I'm his partner.*

He went out on the balcony and burned the single piece of paper, allowing the ashes to blow in the breeze. He returned, unfolded the map, and sat down. The map of Indochina was current with roads, villages, and the cities clearly marked. Charlie stared at it, trying to memorize important parts in case someone took it from him. He studied the topography, learned the population of cities, all to prepare himself. *For what I really do not know yet.*

His thoughts kept returning to the memo, and John Sawyer's real reasons for being here. Counter-espionage, certainly? Translator? Not hardly. Then he had a thought. *He's here to kill someone.*

Charlie wrestled with that idea. *Perfect cover. He would have me unknowingly locate his target, and he would do the rest. Then out of the country as quickly and quietly as he entered under the bogus name. He slid the map under* the bedsprings.

"John Sawyer, assassin," he whispered. *For some inexplicable reason, it all begins to make sense."*

Chapter 16

"**S**orry, that piece on you got censured," Jack said the next time he saw Charlie. "Here's the final edit. He handed a type written page to him. "We had to delete any mention of the CIA, security reasons, so I finished the story. I wanted it to pass the censures."

Charlie reviewed it quickly and saw that everything after his European adventures was gone. In its place was: "I am proud to be serving my country here in South Vietnam to help defeat the Communists."

I was sure you wouldn't mind so I told her to send it."

"Thanks." Charlie was disappointed but not defeated. "Jack, I left a message on your table, something I remembered."

They took the elevator to Jack's room. Charlie noticed that there were no soldiers in the lobby. "Sit down," Jack said. He walked over and picked up the simple folded slip of paper. "This?"

"Yeah," Charlie said. "Something that just occurred to me."

Jack quickly read the message. He turned to look at Charlie. "We're ahead of you, Stanek. Forget this DaLat thing. It was probably a wild goose chase, anyway. I've been putting together an assault force of about a 100-150 soldiers from the National Army, and from Archer's paramilitary force. The general said they were the best of his men."

"What the hell does that mean?"

Jack smiled. "We're going to get our man...and woman."

"Right," Charlie scoffed at the idea. "You're dreaming. They don't know where to look."

"Intelligence, Charlie, intelligence. I've been working on that for two months or more. We got us a papa-son who's talking."

"Tortured him, eh?"

"Be surprised how willing someone is if you hold a gun to his kid's head."

"You're the expert."

Jack ignored the comment. "We got grid coordinates, troops ready to go, air support, and a plan. We hit them in two days, early. The general is on board."

Is he lying? Charlie wondered. Do I take the chance that he is? "Now you only need a war, eh?"

"This is a Vietnamese operation. We're along as advisors."

"I want to see this. I'm going with you," Charlie said.

"The hell you are," Jack replied. "We got you tight here, and looking at you, I'd say you're comfortable."

"If you capture their leaders, what more do you need me for?"

"Good point. This works and we leave for Australia in a week."

"If it doesn't?"

"You're not going anywhere then, buddy," Jack said with a shrug. "So don't pack your bags just yet."

"Jack, do you really plan to capture Le Doan and Madame Thieu, or just shoot them outright," Charlie asked pointedly. "If you captured them, what more do you need? Shoot them and be done with it before they are extradited to the North."

Jack did not reply.

"You not going to answer me, buddy?"

"I think we're done here," Jack said. "Good night."

Charlie left without another word. He's a real talker, he thought. But, if it is true they are planning an attack, how do I get the word out? Bob. He took the elevator to the lobby. Suddenly, it flashed in his mind. Are they allowing me to escape, believing I'll lead them to their camp? Is that why Jack was so loose with the information? He felt trapped, but knew he had to make a decision quickly.

He saw Bob outside waiting for a fare. He knocked on the glass to wave him into the lobby.

"You want taxi, sir?"

Charlie immediately saw the lapse in security. "Bob, 2:00 in the morning behind the opera house," he whispered. I have to force their hand, he decided. "I'm still under house arrest so I can't leave," he said louder.

Bob nodded politely and walked to the desk to speak with the clerk while Charlie disappeared into the dining lounge. He ate and thought everything through. He returned to the lobby in time to see Jack and another American leave the hotel. He thought it was Barton but wasn't certain.

Standing at the lobby window, he saw that the Citroen was gone. The guards were standing around smoking and chatting as if waiting for something to happen. Something's up, he decided. He walked across the lobby, looked out the window onto the terrace, and saw two guards returning to their posts. New orders, he thought. He saw the Captain of the Guards standing in the lobby and approached.

"Are your men sleeping?" he asked

He gave Charlie a hard look. "No sleep," he said. "You sleep now."

"One more week and I go home," he replied. "Good night." He saw the captain from the corner of his eyes watching him enter the elevator.

Back in his room, he began to write a note to Vouc but decided against it. He examined the map one last time, making a mental note of the route, then stashed it in his bag with the money—all the dollars and piaster he could scrape up.

A knock on the door. He slid the bag under the bed and went to open it. "Vouc, he said. "I was hoping it was you."

She entered and kissed him on the cheek."

He kissed her on the mouth while she continued to stand. "Tonight we sit on the terrace, just you and me?" He slowly raised her blouse above her breasts, running his hand down her loose fitting pants to touch her."

She pushed him away. "No Charlie, today I work hard. Tomorrow night." She stepped away, straightening her blouse.

"The guards?"

"The captain took them away from the terrace. All soldiers in front tonight and tomorrow. No problem. We talk tomorrow," she said, distancing herself away from him.

"Ok, tomorrow night. No guards," he said. He knew she was lying. They are there somewhere watching.

"Yes, if you want. I go to bed now."

Then he knew. Vouc is in on it. They want me to leave through the terrace so they can follow. "I see you tomorrow night and we go outside."

"Yes," She turned for the door. "I must go, Charlie, to sleep," she repeated.

"I will sit on the terrace tonight. What else do I have to do," he said smiling. He walked her to the door. She turned to kiss him again, a cold, dispassionate one on the lips. "Good bye, my love," she said. "Think of me when you go." She left.

Charlie tried to get some sleep, but the effort was futile. He paced about the room. No gun, nothing. He worried, but he felt certain they would not shoot him if it came to that.

Early morning came with the hotel dark and quiet. Charlie looked out over the balcony and saw five guards in the dim light. Exiting his room, he took the stairs. At ground level, he made his way out. The terrace was empty and silent as he suspected.

Charlie disappeared into bushes at the edge of the terrace. He figured someone was watching from somewhere, but he was unable to spot them. Entering the street, he stopped to reconnoiter, looking for Bob, and another vehicle he was certain was waiting. He was only a few blocks from the opera house. Time clicked away. He heard no shouting behind him, but that meant nothing.

In front of him, the old opera house rose up in all its majesty. Bob's Citroen parked around the corner, and Charlie made directly for it, sliding in the front passenger seat.

"Where to, Major?" Bob asked, shifting into gear.

"West toward Cambodia," Charlie replied. He looked back and several blocks away he saw headlights come on. "They're tailing us. Speed up."

"No problem," Bob replied, pressing down on the accelerator.

With limited traffic and even fewer pedestrians, they got to the outskirts quickly. Again, Charlie looked back. He thought he still saw headlights.

"Bob, we must get a message through to Truin."

"Message, Major?" He did not understand.

"We must warn Truin that General Duc is planning to attack the base camp. I received important intelligence. With 150 soldiers, they plan to attack tomorrow morning early. We must find a way to get the message through."

"I have friend in Cu Chi. We fight the French together. He can get the message to Truin. I certain."

"Can you shake them off before then?"

Bob smiled. "I have good car. We leave them in dust. Is how you say?"

"You got it."

On open road, narrow and filled with potholes and ruts, the old Citroen sailed. The two men bounced along. Charlie again looked and still saw the headlights.

"I see lights, Bob said, looking in the rearview mirror.

"Good," Charlie replied. "The fools think I'm leading them to some type of rendezvous."

They arrived in Cu Chi in record time. Darkness surrounded them, but they knew dawn would arrive soon. Bob, without headlights, shifted down and turned one corner, then another. After maneuvering, he slowed for a nicely kept stone house near the edge of the village. He pulled in and immediately killed the engine. They saw no other lights near them. Good, Charlie thought.

"Quickly," Charlie said. "They must not lose sight of us for too long."

Bob was confused, but followed his orders. "I give friend message then we go," he said, springing from the car. "You stay."

Within seconds, Bob returned and they were off. "To Cambodia?" he asked.

Charlie looked at him grimly. "No Bob. Take me back to Saigon."

"Saigon? Why, Major? They will capture you."

"If they don't get lost..," he replied with a smile. "I must return to the hotel and pretend I was out for a walk. You will disappear. Stay away from the hotel for a few days."

"Why? We almost to Cambodia?"

"Bob, it's the CIA. They have eyes everywhere and they watch. They would find me there, or in Singapore, or in Australia. Still, they are fools who think they know everything. They hoped I would lead them to Le Doan because they have no spies to tell them where he is, only victims of their torture. That must never happen."

The headlights reappeared behind them.

"Americans..." Bob said, beginning to understand the complexity of the American character. "Not so different from the Vietnamese." He smiled.

"I will find another way to go home."

"You the boss." Bob turned the Citroen around in a small village. They began to retrace their travel back to Saigon. The Jeep passed going in the other direction. Charlie enjoyed seeing that. He hoped they drove another hour or two before they gave up, and realized they were had.

In Saigon as the sun broke the horizon, they drove down the narrow streets, passing vendors setting up their stalls. Nearing the hotel, Charlie said, "Bob let me out where I got in, then go. "You have the money, right?"

"Your money, Major."

"Bob, don't worry. It's the U.S. Government's money."

Bob dropped Charlie off near the opera house. People were already beginning to collect in the streets for another day of survival. Charlie retraced his path onto the terrace. He saw no guards, only the cook. He walked through the unlocked door and across the lobby. He saw Vouc at the desk.

"Good morning," he said pleasantly.

She looked up surprised. "Charlie?" That was all she could say.

"I had a nice walk, Vouc, so I think I will go to my room for a shower. "You didn't rent it to someone else, did you?"

She stared at him, silent.

Chapter 17

Charlie undressed and prepared for a long, late afternoon nap, and then he hoped, a shower. He expected a visit some time later when Jack and Barton realized what had happened, and returned. He slept soundly knowing that he had done all he could to protect Truin from Diem and the CIA.

He stepped out of the shower about middle of the afternoon. No one had disturbed him since his early morning return. He thought that strange, but enjoyed the peaceful sanity the space gave him.

Dressing, he heard a knock at the door. He opened it to one of the hotel clerks. He smiled, bowing politely when Charlie opened the door. The young man handed him a newspaper—*LA Times.*

Betty doesn't forget about me, he thought appreciative. "Thank you," he said, preparing to tip him, but remembered he gave Bob all his money. "Sorry," he shrugged.

He sat and read, finding a section on Betty's reporting about South Vietnam. He found the article on him about the third page in. Not as long as I expected but a good profile of me, he decided.

Further down on the page was a write-up on a battle between Diem's government forces and a sect called Hoa Hoa. According to the author, not Betty, the sect surrendered after a brief battle southwest of Saigon, but their commander, a man named Ba Cut with several thousand men, escaped to the Cambodian border. He saw that the article was from the UPI wire service.

A good distraction, he thought, wondering if General Duc had to move south to command his troops. When he opened the door earlier, he noticed a guard in the hall near his door. He smiled. I think I will sit in the lobby to observe. He wondered when Jack would return. He may still be in Bien Hoa with Barton re-examining their failed plan. Such a foolish gamble. That made him smile again.

I may be able to gather helpful information for when I really must escape my gilded cage, and it's better to develop contacts without the CIA around. He considered his late-night adventure, and desperately hoped Truin had received his message in time for them to escape any attack from Duc's soldiers.

With the newspaper carefully tucked under an arm, he opened the door, nodded politely to the guard, and walked to the elevator.

In the lobby, he looked for Vouc but did not see her. He sat and began reading *The Times* again, always on alert. Soon the Captain of the Guard entered from outdoors. He saw Charlie immediately and walked toward him.

Charlie pretended not to see him. The captain planted himself in front of him. Finally, Charlie looked up. "Captain, how are you?" He remained sitting.

"You…" the captain said in a challenging voice. "Where you go? Not to Viet Minh?"

"Go?" he asked appearing confused. "I've been here all morning."

"Liar," the captain replied with anger. "You leave hotel for long time, maybe five hours. Where you go?"

"A very long walk," he said. "I like your city very much."

The captain turned and left, returning to the front desk in a huff. Charlie, having spent a leisurely afternoon in the lobby, prepared to return to his room, then decided, that since he had not eaten since the previous day, entered the dining lounge. Dinner.

He saw Jacques Chastain across the room. "May I join you?" he asked the reporter.

"Oui, Major. Please."

Charlie ordered his usual—fruit, rice, and tea.

At first Chastain said nothing, content to eat, but Charlie felt his eyes on him. "The French soldiers have gone home," he finally announced.

"Smart," Charlie replied. "I suspect more American soldiers soon. One act is completed and the second act begins, eh?"

"So it would seem."

Charlie received his order and began to eat.

"The National Army has rid itself of the Hoa Hoa sect, driving the remnants into Cambodia. Now only the Communists and the Buddhists stand against him...and the Americans."

"They fought in the delta, I hear," Charlie added. "I thought General Duc and his army were north of Saigon." He finished his meal and waited for Chastain to reply.

"The general sent thousands of his soldiers south to reinforce his units there, but he stayed in DaLat until the fighting was over. Important business, I gather."

"Protecting Bao Dai from the Viet Minh?"

"Ha! Possibly," he said. "But you would know more about that." He smiled at Charlie.

"No one tells me much."

"Yes? I hear your contacts are better than Duc's."

"What else have you heard, Jacques?"

"That you know where the Viet Minh base camp is that everyone searches for. But, oh so romantic, a man in love…you tell them nothing. Then you lead them on—how you say—wild goose chase, eh?"

"You have very good sources."

"Madame Thieu is now in hiding, having escaped the clutches of the evil General Duc. It is such a story, and you, Major, are the story's hero," Chastain said, smitten with his own illusions of love.

"I'm looking for a ride home. Can you help me?"

"To leave paradise and its beauties behind?"

"I'm ready, and frankly, I can't seem to grasp all the subterfuge here."

"I understand completely, Major. But first, my story must continue a while longer."

Charlie prepared to leave.

"Please, sit a while longer," Chastain said, wanting to speak. "The Viet Minh are a formidable force. We French learned that the hard way. How long will it take you Americans?" he said on a more serious note.

"We're not very good at history. Americans always march to the beat of progress trying to shape a different future, but progress has its down side, I think."

"Sadly, yes." Chastain leaned forward. "Major, what's your role here? That's not clear to me."

"I have no role and have requested they send me home, but, as I'm currently under house arrest, they want to keep me here."

"Maybe you know too much, eh?"

"Yet obviously not enough," Charlie replied. "And Jacques, I cannot accept our role here. It hurts to see us make a terrible mistake, and destroy this beautiful land."

"I think the Americans have found their horse, and plan to ride him to the end. Yes, that's what I hear from your new ambassador."

"I haven't met him."

Chastain paused as if trying to make a decision. "Major, I plan a trip to Can Tho in a couple of days. Why don't you join me?"

"I would like that," he replied. Anything to get out of here. "I will need clearance from the Ambassador."

"I think I can manage that." He stood. "Remember—three days and we leave early."

"We'll probably have to take my aide along. We're inseparable these days."

"CIA? I understand." Chastain stood, shook Charlie's hand and left.

Charlie stayed awhile, sipping his tea. Will they allow me on this trip outside the hotel even with Jack along? I wonder how to convince them.

He knocked on Jack's door, hoping he had returned. The door opened and to Charlie's surprise, Jack greeted him. "Hi Jack, where you been?" He asked. "I've been waiting for you. Get lost?"

"Go to hell," He tried to slam the door but Charlie positioned himself in the threshold.

"Let's talk," Charlie said, pushing the door open wider. Jack finally let him in.

"You think I'm so stupid I don't know what you did?"

"I've been wondering."

"We never believed you'd lead us directly to their base camp."

"Why'd you set me up, allow me to escape?" Charlie asked. "You thought I'd take you there."

"Hell no. We want your contacts, the people here who can take you to them," Jack said. "You know what? We got what we wanted."

"What do you mean?"

"The guy you call Bob. We suspected he was a Commie or at least a Viet Minh sympathizer. It would have been better if we caught a couple of others, but he'll do. When I'm done with him, he'll be singing like a canary. It may take one hour or one year, but he'll talk, and then we'll have the whole network."

Charlie was silent.

"You knew we were trailing you, didn't you? How?"

"I've been around, Jack. Everything that day smelled set-up."

"My Vietnamese trainees are learning fast and they have a fondness for torture," Jack said, darkness shrouding his college boy features. "Can Bob drive taxi with one hand? What do you think?"

"Jack or John or whatever your real name is. I thought you had a special skill like languages, weapons, but you are nothing but a sadistic killer. That's why you're here doing the job you do. You're waiting for me to lead you to a target, aren't you?"

"Fuck you," he growled. He sat down and motioned for Charlie to sit. "Let's talk, Stanek. You want your freedom, and I want to know real fast where that base camp is."

"Let's hear it."

"You tell me—show me—on a map where they are and you are good to go."

Charlie was not expecting or prepared to negotiate a deal. Who do I betray, he thought.

"Think Stanek. I don't have all night."

"What about your other intel? I thought Duc was attacking tomorrow morning?"

"He got sidetracked and is down in the delta."

Charlie was surprised to get that out of him. "You let Bob go now and I'll tell you what I know."

"Everything?"

"Yeah, get your map," he said, giving in. I cannot let them hurt Bob. Everything he did for me."

"You have my word he will be freed as soon as I get to Bien Hoa."

"Ok, I trust your word." What choice do I have, he thought, feeling trapped.

Jack retrieved his map, unfolded it on the bed.

Charlie bent over it. "I can't give you grid coordinates. I only know what I walked and saw."

"I understand."

"Here, right about here," he said, placing his forefinger where he thought the base camp was.

"I'm heading to get Archer now. You better be close or your contact is raw meat for my boys." He folded the map and prepared to leave.

Charlie, angry at the decision he had to make, also got up to leave. He returned to his room while Jack ran down the stairs. Opening the door, he saw a note on the floor.

"Vouc? He wondered, reaching down to pick it up. He looked around for a guard but none was present. He entered and closed the door. He carefully unfolded it, not knowing who or what. He read, *Safe. Love you, Truin.* Charlie breathed a long sigh of relief.

Chapter 18

Charlie learned from Jack two days later that they found the base camp. A short fire fight had ensued with casualties on each side. With air support and heavier weapons, the National Army supported by the American advisors including Jack, eventually gained the upper hand. The Viet Minh fighters withdrew into the jungle, after suffering many casualties. Jack told him that they had a number of prisoners to interrogate. He seemed happy about that. Did they expect to capture Le Doan and Truin? he wondered. In any case, Jack said nothing about that.

That same day, he saw Bob through the lobby window standing by his Citroen. Charlie smiled. Jack has some integrity, he thought. He sat in the lobby. Jack had mysteriously disappeared without a word after their chance meeting. Charlie knew that if Jack was gone longer than 24 hours he would leave a message at the desk for him. There was no message.

Vouc was keeping her distance from him, which was okay with Charlie. He had little use for traitors. The captain had removed his guards from the grounds and Charlie was free to come and go as he pleased. That's something, he decided.

Now what? He asked himself. Colonel Archer sent him word that the new Ambassador wants to meet him. He looked forward to the afternoon meeting. He hoped this meant he could finally get out and return to Australia. Then there was that trip to Can Tho with the French journalist. He could almost look forward to it after all that had happened.

He took a taxi—not Bob's—to the temporary American embassy. He was immediately ushered to the Ambassador's office. Charlie was surprised, as he did not know what kind of reception he would receive.

The Ambassador stood to greet him. "Well, the only American in South Vietnam who knows anything about the Vietnamese," he said, smiling broadly. He was a tall man—as tall as Charlie—but much older, with greying hair and a very personable smile. Magnetic, Charlie would describe it. "Please sit. We must talk."

Charlie sat. A Vietnamese employee served coffee. He did not speak, choosing to allow the Ambassador to initiate.

"Tell me about your mission here, Major."

Charlie told him that he understood his mission was to find a suitable replacement for Prime Minister Diem. "That has obviously changed. Now, I have no mission," he told the Ambassador with a forced look of disappointment.

The Ambassador laughed, a hearty not faked laugh. "We all have a mission, major: to help build a democratic state here. I think you can support that."

"A democracy? Of course, I can support that, but...

"Good, good," he said interrupting, but with the enduring smile again.

"Sir," Charlie began. "I was initially told I would be here only several weeks. I have a young son back home without a mother. I need to get back to him."

"I understand you're living in Australia, married an Australian woman?"

"That's correct. She passed several years back—cancer."

"I see the urgency of your return and will do all I can to facilitate that."

Thank you," Charlie said. He was sensing the meeting was going well.

"But Major, I have one request before you leave." He moved closer to Charlie.

"Sir?"

"The Frenchman, Jacques Chastain, I believe you know is traveling to Can Tho tomorrow."

"Yes he is."

"I want you to accompany him," he said. "See what you think of Diem's army. He recently won a battle against one of the sects there, a battle Colonel Archer is raving about. Battle-ready and all that. Observe them and pump the journalist for his thoughts on the present situation here. I think that you and he may be the only objective eyes in the whole damn country."

No smile, but his brows furled, Charlie saw. This guy is good. "An objective opinion, sir? Free from the U.S. Army here?"

"Yes, I want to know about Colonel Archer's para military soldiers that he speaks so glowingly about. How do they hold up...in your opinion? They are around Can Tho, I understand."

"I can do that."

"I know you can, Major. I have read your file and am especially interested in your work with the Central European partisans. Your superior at the time, Colonel Donovan, provided outstanding remarks about you. Yes, he did." Again the smile that consumed everything in the room. A real politician, Charlie thought.

"I'll need an interpreter. Someone I can trust."

"You'll have him, and the Frenchman tells me he speaks passable Vietnamese."

"I'm prepared to leave early tomorrow morning."

"Excellent," he said, standing and extending his hand. "Report back to me, me Major, no one else, when you return."

"Yes, sir."

The road near Can Tho was rough and clogged with pedestrians, many fleeing the recent fighting there. It took all morning to reach the city. Jacques, Charlie, and a young man the Embassy had assigned him as interpreter rode in an older American Ford with their Vietnamese driver.

Charlie and Jacques spoke at great length of Europe. Charlie was most interested in how things had changed since the end of the war.

"Even West Germany is prospering," Jacques said.

Soon they were on a complicated, yet more relevant topic—the Cold War struggle between the United States and the Soviet Union. They covered the People's Republic of China finally, but neither man seemed to know much about the Chinese.

They arrived in the city amidst a large crowd gathered to watch the National Army troops march prisoners through the main thoroughfare. Charlie spied General Duc in his Jeep not far from where they parked the Ford. All three got out and began to move through the crowd.

"Jacques, shall we speak with the general?" Charlie asked. He pointed to the Vietnamese officer standing only meters away from them.

"I know him well," Jacques replied. They approached him.

"General Duc," Charlie called. The general saw them and smiled pleasantly. He did not move.

"General, may we speak about your victory here?" Jacques asked, speaking Vietnamese.

Without a word, Duc looked hard at Charlie. "With this Communist?" he asked with a scowl.

Charlie considered Duc's attempt at an insult a badge of honor. Jacques fought to hold back a smile.

"With me, General," Jacques said with an appropriate measure of respect. "I am doing a story on the National Army for Le Monde. I would like to ask you about your battle here against the Hoa Hao sect."

"Not with him," Duc replied.

"Major Stanek has other business. He will not join us."

"Come, we speak over there." He motioned to a larger concrete building with a tile roof and thatched overhang. Only his soldiers were present outside, mostly sitting in the shade.

Charlie understood completely, and did not really want to engage with the general. "Come," he said to his interpreter. "We speak with the soldiers and their officers."

Charlie spent the next several hours speaking with soldiers. He found higher-ranking officers who described the fighting in glowing terms, of course. "A great victory," each of them said. Charlie learned that the Hoa Hao leaders with several thousand armed men had safely fled across the border into Cambodia, out of reach. "They will launch raids across the border, so we must move further north to combat them," a ranking officer told him. "After our battle with the Viet Minh, we will be prepared there, too."

Charlie inquired about the local militia forces and they directed him to a compound on the outskirts of the city. Attempting to enter the compound, a young man partially clothed in fatigues, wearing sandals, halted them. The man spoke with his interpreter while Charlie looked him over. His rifle was ancient, probably of French design, he decided. A large brimmed hat, woven from rice straw sat atop his head. Worse of all in Charlie's mind, the young man demonstrated no military bearing at all. "I want to speak with the man in charge here," he directed his interpreter.

The young man nodded and led them to a bunker on the far side of the compound. Charlie noticed much of the high dirt berm was recently constructed. Several men sat on top, also armed with outdated weapons. He saw nothing heavier than rifles. An older man dressed similarly to the others came out of the sandbagged bunker to greet them. The place reminded Charlie of the local force compound in Duc Trong. The men here were more poorly armed, and he saw no American advisors present.

The man, ranking noncommissioned officer at the compound, invited them inside for tea. He seemed friendly and open. Charlie, explaining he was a major in the United States Army. He told him, the American government sent him to Vietnam to learn about the soldiers here. The sergeant was very forthcoming, explaining that he had fought with the French. He said he did not know much about the new government, and he was curious as to why someone had divided Vietnam into two parts.

His primary concern seemed to be his family and community, Charlie wrote in the margin of his notebook. He also told Charlie that neither he nor his men had received any training from anyone since '49. He considered that an ominous sign if the government wanted to extend control over the area.

"You are American?" he asked. "Why are you in Vietnam?"

Charlie was hard-pressed to answer that question. "To help you," he finally replied.

"To help us do what?" the man asked.

That stumped him. "To protect you." Charlie figured if he said 'from the Communists,' the man would have no idea about what he was talking.

"More modern weapons, machine guns," the man implored Charlie repeatedly during their conversation. He was polite and overly respectful throughout his visit, and he seemed to appreciate that Charlie inquired.

They returned to the Ford to find Jacques and the driver waiting. On the long drive back to Saigon, they spoke of what each had learned. Charlie omitted telling the Frenchman how he had found the local militia, only that they had added little to the fighting.

"The Army received training from the Americans, who I also was able to speak with," Jacques said. "It was they who called in the air strikes from Bien Hoa. Duc said the airplanes were powerful weapons. He bragged that with them we will soon control all of South Vietnam."

The French must have already supplied the planes and pilot training, Charlie decided. The American advisors have not been here long enough to train pilots.

Very late when they returned, Charlie decided to wait until morning to brief the Ambassador. He checked at the front desk for a message from Jack. None and he saw that Jack had not picked up his earlier message. *That is curious*, he thought. He also inquired about Co Vouc.

"She go," was all the clerk said.

Charlie returned to his room, feeling exhausted. To rest his long legs, he stretching out on the bed. The balcony doors were wide open, allowing the noise to enter with the breeze. He easily heard the cars below. He began to write up his notes of the day's activities to present in the morning to the Ambassador.

Still, Jack was not far from his mind. *The first weeks here, I could not shake him, but now I cannot find him. He considered knocking on his door but decided against it. Why do I care?* He was not interrogating Truin.

Chapter 19

Charlie walked into the Ambassador's suite of offices early. The first person he saw in the reception area was Colonel Archer. "Colonel, you're up early?" Charlie said in passing.

Archer immediately stood. "Why didn't Stover accompany you to Can Tho. I ordered him to," he said in Charlie's face.

"Ask the Ambassador." Charlie wondered if Archer would meet the Ambassador with him or later. He preferred later.

"Where the hell is he?" Archer asked. "Have you spoken with him recently?"

"Colonel, I haven't seen Jack in at least two days. "I figured he was working with you torturing prisoners or what not."

"Fuck you," Archer whispered with growing anger. He returned to his chair.

The young Vietnamese receptionist watched the two aghast, but luckily not understanding much of the conversation.

"Major, I've been expecting your visit," The Ambassador said by way of a greeting. "I waited last night, but I know it was a long drive. Please sit and tell me what you have discovered."

Charlie sat, pulled out his carefully copied page of notes, and began his briefing. The older man listened intently with his head tilted to one side and resting in the palm of his hand.

"First of all, the air strikes were very effective in turning the tide of battle," Charlie began. "The National Army soldiers seemed upbeat and motivated. Morale from my observation appeared good. I saw that most carried American arms, all had uniforms, and they appeared disciplined. I saw much destruction but no pillaging from the soldiers."

The Ambassador nodded.

"The general was in control, but no one seems to have any idea of the nature of the forces they soon may be up against." Charlie threw the latter statement out there, thinking of the Communists.

The Ambassador seemed to understand, mumbling, "The Commies," but continued listening without interruption.

Charlie finally filled him in on the details Jacques had learned and provided him. When he had completed that part of his briefing, he paused to allow the Ambassador time for questions and clarifications, which he did at great length. Charlie was impressed with his knowledge of the situation, indicated by the insightful questions he asked.

"On many of your questions, sir, I must defer to Colonel Archer and his team. My only experiences here have been limited to DaLat and Can Tho."

"What about the local militia forces?"

"Yes, sir. I was told by the NCO in charge of the compound there, that they did not participate in the fighting against the Hoa Hao."

The Ambassador shook his head.

"Sir, the situation there as I saw it is a completely different story."

"Go on."

"Weapons were old, nothing heavier than old French rifles, and the men had little in the way of uniforms. Worse of all, there was no military discipline exhibited by any of the militiamen I saw. The motivation to engage the enemy I found among the Czechs was nonexistent in Can Tho. The NCO said neither he nor his men had received any training in at least six years."

"I see. These are issues that must be addressed."

"Sir, the sergeant told me he did not understand that the Americans were helping, and was only superficially aware that Bao Dai headed the government of a divided Vietnam. He asked about the French. I felt it unnecessary to broach the subject of Communism, believing he had no idea about what I was talking. With updated weapons and training, I would suggest General Duc indoctrinate his soldiers."

"I agree, Major."

"I think Colonel Archer has much work to do."

"Yes, yes, we have work to do," the Ambassador repeated as a way to conclude the briefing. "Thank you, Major. You have been most helpful. Colonel Archer is waiting as we speak, so I will brief him on your report and see how he responds."

"I might add, sir, that the Frenchman was very helpful. I told him nothing about my findings on the militia. His story will focus on his interview with General Duc."

"Smart, Major." He stood and extended his hand. "Again, thank you. Please tell the colonel to come in."

Charlie did not bother to renew his request to leave country ASAP, believing the Ambassador, not wanting to deal with the subject, would put him off.

Opening the door to his room, Charlie saw a note slid under the door. Jack? He opened it and read. "Charlie, I miss you. Is Vouc taking care of you? We will soon be together when it is safe." He considered its meaning, and then walked over to destroy the small, folded paper by tearing it up and flushing it.

An unexpected knock on the door. Charlie strolled over to answer it, not knowing whom to expect, but still hoping it was Jack.

The housekeeping woman stood in front of him, very excited. No thanks, he was about to say but the woman was pointing.

"Come, come," she said in a rapid burst of English.

Charlie thought he saw fear in her eyes. He followed as she led him to Jack's room. The door was wide open and she pointed to the floor beside a chair.

He walked over to where she pointed. "Jack!" he exclaimed, visually shaken to see him lying on the floor. He froze, then quickly bent over him. He checked his pulse, his mouth for any visible sign of life. "Dead," Charlie finally whispered.

The woman stood behind him not moving but watching. She nodded when she realized he was dead.

He again examined the body. Stiff, curled up in a fetal position. Vomit was on the floor near his mouth, foam on his lips. A seizure? Heart attack? He could not tell but immediately suspected foul play. Dead for maybe 24 hours, he quickly guessed. Continuing his examination, Charlie next looked at the dead man's fingers. He saw white lines across the nails. He leaned closer sniffing around his mouth, and caught a whiff of something that smelled like garlic. He began to suspect a heavy dose or doses of arsenic, something he had experience with in his work as a deep cover agent.

Jack was fully clothed and appeared to be preparing to leave. Charlie searched his pockets, finding nothing out of the ordinary. A passport under the name of Jack Stover and a single slip of paper only. He unfolded it and saw only a nine-digit number. He slid that paper into his pocket without the woman seeing. He needed to look at it more closely.

Charlie searched the room while the woman still stood there frozen. He found nothing. His clothing and his satchel lie on the bed. A partially eaten meal was on the bedside table. He smelled the remainder of the seafood and rice meal. He caught a feint yet similar odor.

Still searching, he opened the satchel and found another passport buried deep in a side pocket. This passport was under the name John Sawyer.

I have to notify someone but who? Barton? With the woman still frozen her spot by the door, he walked over to touch her arm. "We go," he told her. He knew he had to contact the Americans.

"No talk," he ordered the woman. They left, closing the door behind them. Charlie marched through the lobby without speaking to anyone. He ran out of the building. He hoped Barton was nearby.

He marched into the CIA station out of breath. "Where's Barton?" he asked a young American civilian sitting behind the desk. "It's an emergency. I must speak with him at once."

"Yes, sir." The young man picked up the phone and called a number. "Sir, a man here to speak with you. He says it's urgent." He looked up at Charlie. "Name?"

"Major Charles Stanek."

"Yes, sir." He handed the phone to Charlie.

"It's Stover, Jack Stover," he blurted out. "He's dead."

Charlie stood in the room while four American soldiers with Barton moved Jack's body. They placed it in a body bag then lifting him onto a cart. He had told Barton nothing of what he had discovered earlier during his search, but he handed Barton both passports.

"Take him to Bien Hoa, prepare to fly him to Guam where he will be autopsied" Barton ordered the soldiers. He looked at Charlie. "We need to search the room, Major."

Together they thoroughly search of the room, but uncovered nothing that Charlie had not already seen. "What's your opinion?" Barton asked Charlie.

"He was poisoned."

Barton stopped what he was doing, turned and stared, at him. "You sound damn definite."

"I saw symptoms of arsenic on him, and I'd advise you to test the food over there. He pointed to the partially eaten meal still on the bedside table. "I've had some experience with poisons."

"Sergeant, bag the food and we'll take it to Bien Hoa. Someone there can test it."

"Anything else on your mind?"

"Yeah, why two passports if he was here on primarily an advisory mission? That doesn't make much sense."

Barton nodded but said nothing.

Charlie escorted him downstairs.

"I'll let you know what we find, Major."

"I'm coming with you." Charlie already knew he would gain nothing more by further examination of Jack's room.

"No, you've done everything you can," he replied. "I'll notify family."

"His family?" Charlie repeated. "I don't know anything about him, only that he was working in Australia, and he was not married."

"I'll take care of it," Barton said. "We'll talk later." He turned to leave, and Charlie left standing there. He turned to walk back to the elevator, and saw Vouc standing at her usual place behind the desk. She watched him.

He walked over.

"Charlie?" she asked. "What happened?"

"Jack. He's dead."

"Dead? How?"

"Heart attack." Others in the lobby, mostly Vietnamese were trying to listen to the conversation.

"Oh, so young," she said in a voice with no emotion. "I cannot believe it."

Charlie shrugged.

"Charlie, please come tonight," she whispered. "I've missed you."

He smiled and walked toward the elevator. He heard Vouc speaking loudly to the others standing around the desk.

Jack poisoned, he thought as the doors closed. *Was he a threat to someone, and had to be silenced.* He tried to make sense of that.

He entered his room, closed the door and locked it. He walked over to his bed to retrieve the map. He reached into a front pocket to get the slip of paper with the numbers. *Just a hunch*, he thought, unfolding the map. He examined both closely. "Right about there." Using the numbers as grid coordinates, he quickly saw that everything lined up. He positioned his finger on the map at a location southwest of the one he already provided Jack several days earlier. This coordinate was in Bien Phuoc province near the Cambodian border, or northwest of Saigon. An easy drive from Bien Hoa.

Hmm, interesting, he thought, and filed the location away for further reference. Barton should also have it. Their interrogation appears effective. He folded the map and again hid it. He stood on the balcony considering what he had learned. He knew it would be important to Truin's survival. Was Jack planning some type of assassination attempt on the Viet Minh leadership? Yet Truin could easily flee to safety across the border. *I think an assassination attempt*, he finally decided. With General Duc's troop in the vicinity, he could pull it off.

A team carefully and silently approaches, sets up, and waits for an opportunity, often waiting for hours. He considered. That requires careful planning and a guide to get you there without discovery, but most importantly—it demands excellent intelligence. Positioning, daily movements, and escape routes had to be carefully worked out. The sophistication, brashness, and commitment defied his assessment of the Americans here.

"If I'm correct, I am very impressed," he said softly. "Do they fly in another shooter?" He asked no one.

He knocked on Vouc's door. The hour was late, the usual time for their rendezvous. The door opened immediately. She evidently expected him, dressed in her robe with the dragon prints, and Charlie knew, nothing underneath.

Vouc kissed him lightly on the cheek—a cold meaningless peck. "Come in," she whispered. "I wait for you."

Charlie walked in, closed the door, and followed her. He had become unsure about this young woman during the last several days, and so, knew he had to be careful.

She led him to her bed. "Where have you been, Charlie?" she asked and began to undress him.

He slowly pulled the sash and her robe fell open. He slid it off her and let it drop to the floor. Charlie rubbed his hands softly across her shoulders, delicately touching her breasts while she unbuckled his trousers. "I've looked for you all day," he whispered, then lifted her small breast to touch with his tongue. It was all becoming much too mechanical, The passion had gone.

Vouc responded to his touch, but the urgency was lost. "Hotel business, she whispered. "I out of town. She groaned softly as he worked his magic with his fingers. He laid her gently on the bed.

They made love, a fast lovemaking that lacked the passion they had earlier felt for each other. Those few short days apart had changed everything and they both recognized it.

When finished, they lay together. "So sorry about your friend," she said, but not looking at him.

"He was not my friend, but his death is tragic and sad. So young," Charlie said. "But now I'm free to return to my home. My work here is over." He wanted her to understand that it was over between Vouc and him.

"Yes, I understand. We must part," Vouc said. "Soon, I must go to Paris to marry. I cannot control this arrangement. The general is too powerful." She finally turned to look at him. Vouc softly touched his face. "Charlie, I will remember you and our days together always." She kissed him. "Now you safe and free to return to your home."

A farewell kiss, Charlie decided. Her marriage plans surprised him, especially about going to Paris. "What about Truin?"

"Truin?" The question seemed to surprise her. "She is safe but will never return to Saigon until after elections. I know this."

"So you will leave her behind...with the hotel?"

"Only short trip, then I return."

Charlie did not believe her about the Paris marriage, but didn't press it. "Is Truin still in danger?" he asked, hoping for some insight.

"No longer, but she cannot return to Saigon."

Charlie dressed quietly and left Vouc while she slept. He expected never to have another night with her again. Earlier, he believed he understood the young woman, but now, he had his doubts. *One thing was certain*, he decided. *She is one complicated person, and a very smooth operator. She reminded him of Marta, of Prague, who helped him avoid the Russians. She, too, had her own agenda, her way to survive the politics engulfing her. First with the Nazis and later the Russians.*

Back in his room, Charlie sat and considered again Jack's tragic death. Anyone could have administered the poison slowly or in one massive dose, he concluded. He was learning quickly that here politics was a dangerous sport and fatal. Who? He asked himself. Truin? Yet, how would she know his plan? She is out in the jungle, but she would know how to get to him. He finally understood he had to learn more about Jack's real assignment in Vietnam. For that, he needed to speak to Agent Barton.

Chapter 20

Days passed slowly for Charlie, feeling trapped, with not even the mission to occupy his time and attention. He waited with growing impatience for Barton to contact him regarding Jack's death. He had not seen Vouc since their late night encounter. He could only assume that Truin was still safe in their new hideout.

He decided a long walk was in order. Leaving the hotel, he spied Bob standing next to his Citroen, a few more dents and scrapes graced the vehicle's fenders. Bob saw him and waved him over.

Greeting Bob with a bow and handshake, Charlie thought Bob looked older, wearier. He wondered if the taxi driver was involved in too many extracurricular activities. "How is business?" he asked.

"Slow, he replied. "No one visit Vietnam. Only soldiers come now. Too many troubles, I think."

"Take me for a ride to Vung Tao," Charlie said. "I'm still getting paid, but have nothing to do."

"Ok, boss." Bob opened the door and Charlie slid in.

"We can talk, ok?"

"Yes, much to talk about," he replied. "What happened to American friend?"

Charlie considered how to reply to his question. "Poisoned, I think." He watched for Bob's reaction, suspecting he could be complicit in his death.

Bob looked up at his passenger in the rear view. "Poisoned? Who you think?"

"I don't know," Charlie said. "Have you heard about his death?"

"No, I know nothing, Major," he replied quickly. "No one tell me."

Charlie wanted to believe him. "Any ideas about who may be behind it?"

"Poison," he repeated. "In Vietnam, it common. Rich prefer it to guns."

"In the world of espionage it is also very common. Clean, silent, and hard to trace."

"Spies kill and want to disappear, I think."

Charlie shrugged. "What else can you tell me?"

They had left the city and traveled east to the coastal town. Charlie had been there before, ten years earlier. He remembered it as a beautiful seaside town with long glorious beaches. Bob had told him then that the Vietnamese people are indifferent to sitting on the sand and tanning. Having pure white skin was the fashion goal for the women. That made their beaches more private and secluded for foreigners to enjoy. He liked that, unlike in the U.S. and Australia where they were often crowded with sun worshippers.

"Major, I have message from number one son," he said softly, as if someone else could over hear him.

"What is it?"

"Madame come to my house tomorrow late night. She come for meeting."

"That sounds dangerous for her. Why take such a risk?" he asked concerned.

"Ah Major, she wants to see you. You come? I take you, yes?"

"I'll come," Charlie finally replied. "What about the army searching for her? And the Americans?"

"No problem. The army busy. And the Americans?" He shrugged.

"Does she come alone?"

"No, she protected and many friends watch."

"I'll come."

Charlie and Bob passed most of the day in Vung Tao, walking along the long strand of beach and talking. He learned much about the taxi driver, and as he discovered, an officer with the Viet Minh during their long war with the French. They had wounded him several times, the last seriously. He drove taxi during that period often as cover for his activities, he told Charlie.

Bob's assistance to Charlie proved invaluable ten years ago. Charlie had chased a Japanese war criminal, Captain Suzuki, who had escaped capture by fleeing toward the border. They had to fight but finally apprehended him in the Central highlands of Vietnam. Bob with Charlie, another American, and a Japanese police man caught him. They rode in the same Citroen Bob now drove, and Charlie saw, still proudly displayed the bullet holes stitched across the passenger side of the vehicle.

They returned to Dragon House under cover of darkness, late into the evening. Charlie paid Bob well for his service and entered the hotel. Still, no sign of Vouc. He checked his mailbox, hoping for something from Barton. He was disappointed.

Charlie went to Bien Hoa the next morning determined to speak with Barton, who had neglected to brief him on the progress of the investigation. Bob drove him, not appearing concerned that he had been interrogated only days earlier. *Things are changing*, he thought, or Bob is just gutsy.

Bob passed through the gate with no apparent hassles and delivered him to the American compound. Barton was there, as if expecting him. He immediately ushered Charlie into an office. They were alone.

"You were right. Arsenic," he said as a greeting. "The autopsy verified it."

Charlie thought Barton seemed preoccupied. "Who?" he asked.

"We notified his family. Told them it was a heart attack."

"I figured that already," Charlie replied. "But who?" he repeated.

The agent paused, a long hesitation, before he finally spoke. "We're investigating it as a fatality—murder, but it has been ruled an accident. Washington's orders"

"Any leads?"

"I think the Viet Minh did it or had it done. They have the means and the motive for doing it. Agents here in the city. Not difficult for them to pull off."

"Why kill Stover?" Charlie asked, confused. "He was here as my aide and as an advisor to the Army, like 350 other Americans."

Barton again gave Charlie a hard look, pausing before he answered. "He had another assignment."

"Yeah? What was it?"

"He was ordered to eliminate the Viet Minh leadership in the South to reduce the threat, something we are all tasked with. Now, as Diem consolidates power it is critical."

"An assassin," Charlie said directly and bluntly.

"Major, that is a baseless assumption. You don't know that." Barton seemed more resigned than angry that Charlie made that statement.

"You're his supervisor here. Don't you know his mission?" He's covering something up, Charlie decided. "He went with General Duc's men to attack the Viet Minh camp, didn't he?"

Barton looked hard at Charlie. "That was his mission, yes," he said slowly. "What else can you tell me?"

"He was detached here from Taiwan by Washington, an independent operator. He had his orders from them. I hoped he kept me abreast of his activities, but…"

"Them? Who are them?" Charlie knew from experience how this often worked.

"The CIA."

"That tells me nothing," Charlie replied, feeling frustrated.

"I'm under no orders, Major, to tell you anything about his death."

"What kind of work did he do in Taiwan?"

"Hell, he speaks Chinese, was born there. He monitored radio traffic off the mainland."

"Perhaps, he did more there than monitor radio traffic."

"What does that mean?"

"Hell, I don't know," Charlie replied. "I only met him a couple of days before embarking for Saigon." He saw that Barton was nervous—fig ding with papers on his desk.

Charlie said nothing, waiting…

"Listen," Barton finally said. "I got orders from the Ambassador and signed off on by Colonel Archer to send you home." He held them up. "Pack your bags, Major. You are leaving in a few days."

"That's all you're going to tell me?"

"Have a good flight home. You've been requesting it for months. Here's the order." He handed it to Charlie.

Charlie took his time to read it. *They want to get rid of me,* he thought. *And quickly.* "Hey, this is a manifest for Washington not Sydney."

Barton shrugged. "Don't worry," he hissed. "They probably only want to debrief you."

Secretive bastards, he thought, standing.

Late, Bob picked him up at the hotel for his meeting with Truin. The darkness grew deeper as they drove further into the poorer sections of Saigon. When they arrived at Bob's house, he drove the car into a very secluded spot and they both got out.

"Come," Bob said. He led Charlie through a small-enclosed backyard strewn with auto parts. They entered the house, made of brick, block and thatch, like millions of others in Indochina. The rear of their home was dark. Charlie smelled cooking oil and heard water boiling. The other room in the two-room home was larger. One candle burned in a corner on a three feet long alter. Incense burners, and pictures hung above it.

Seeing was difficult but he heard movement, and then saw several figures. They watched him.

"Sit Major," Bob ordered. "I will get tea for you."

"Thanks," he replied, sitting on a wood chair offered to him by a figure in the shadows.

Quiet reigned while Bob prepared tea. Charlie did not know if Bob's wife was present or not.

"Tea," Bob offered

Charlie saw four small ceramic cups. He took one.

Someone moved toward him, then kneeled beside him. "Charlie," the voice said, taking his hand. Truin.

He looked at her in the darkness. She was dressed in khaki and black. Her hair was tied and she held a wide straw hat in her other hand. "Truin," Charlie whispered. "I thought I'd never see you again."

She squeezed his hand. "We must speak but later." Truin whispered. "Now, we look for medicines." A conversation began which Charlie was not a part of, as voices—male and female-- spoke in the dark. He quietly sipped the tea.

When the lengthy discussion was completed and some kind of decision was made, Truin turned to Charlie.

"Many problems living in the jungle. Malaria, dysentery, very bad. The attack by the army wounded several of our best men. We must buy medicine but where?"

"I see the problem," Charlie agreed. "Truin, two things I must tell you."

"Yes, my love." She leaned closer to give him her full attention.

"I am ordered to leave in a few days, but more importantly for you, the Army has the coordinates for your hiding place near Cambodia."

Truin nodded. "Thank you for the intelligence, but we already have learned the Army found someone to talk to them. We know her well. She is a traitor like many in my country."

Charlie smiled.

"You leave? Must you?"

"I'm being sent to Washington. They say my work here is completed."

"Your son?"

He shrugged. "I must get back to him somehow."

"Will you ever come back to me?" she asked, holding his arm in hers.

"We must say good-bye tonight, Truin."

"I am so sad."

"Can you send letters to me? Through Vouc?"

"No, I cannot trust her, and I tell her nothing," Truin said sharply. "Her friends are not good. They are too friendly with Americans and to General Duc. Soon, she leaves the country. I hear this."

"To Paris, she said."

"Paris?" She looked at Charlie with surprise.

"To get married to General Duc's son."

"Ha! She never marry him. Like a free bird, she goes everywhere, but never tell me. Always like this."

"She has all your money, the hotel, so she can afford to travel."

"Charlie, we have no money, only hotel now. Vouc take money from rich friends and others. She live dangerous life, more than mine, I think."

That surprised Charlie.

"Do not trust her. She niece—family--but...When she say she go to Paris to get married, she lie to you."

"But your message asking if Vouc was taking care of me?"

"I want her to look after you only. Maybe she sleep with you. She likes men, many men. Friends in Saigon talk of this."

Truin, a revolutionary and her niece part of the jet set. Or perhaps, just a whore. He shook his head.

Truin rested her head on Charlie's arm. "Not important because I know I have your heart."

"You will always have my heart."

"Truin, I must ask. Did you have Jack poisoned?"

"It had to be done, but I did not order it. Russian friends who know about him say he is a dangerous man who threatens Le Doan. They have people in Vietnam to help us, they say."

Bob interrupted their conversation. "We must go soon," he said.

They nodded. "Truin, I will give you my address in Australia. In several weeks, a month, I will return there. We can't lose each other."

"You will always be here," she said, her hand on her heart.

They parted. Truin and Charlie said their farewells sadly, but hopeful they would see each other again. She and five others disappeared into the darkness while Charlie rode back to Dragon House with Bob.

Vouc used me, he thought on the ride back. *Gathering information for personal use, and probably selling it to the highest bidder.* He considered whether she helped the Russians and Hanoi to get rid of Jack.

Chapter 21

Charlie was the only passenger on the military transport destined for Guam, Hickam Field, Travis Air Base near San Francisco, a two-day break, then finally on to Andrews AB outside Washington by way of St. Louis. He knew he would probably never see Truin again. That made him very sad, but he was relieved to get the hell out of Saigon. *I hope my stay in Washington will be short. I tell them I don't know a damn thing, do not understand politics in South Vietnam, and have taken no sides,* he decided somewhere between Hickam Field and Travis. Charlie figured the CIA knew more about why Jack Stover or John Sawyer was murdered than he did.

A man he did not recognize greeted him with a simple "Major Stanek, follow me." He whisked him away in a dark Ford. The man drove and spoke not a word to Charlie.

Washington was as he remembered it from earlier days. A typical hot July day and was as steamy as Saigon. Mostly men in their suits marched up the streets hurrying somewhere.

For Charlie ranching sheep was a better and probably more honest occupation.

They parked in front of a nondescript six-story office building in the heart of the city and both men got out, Charlie following the other man into the huge building. They easily passed through security with both men presenting credentials. Looking around and down the deep corridors, green and cold, he saw that the place was also as he remembered it.

The driver left as soon as he parked Charlie in a smaller room, with few furnishings but a table and three chairs. A folder and several pens lay out with military precision on the government-issued table.

He smiled. *Just like in the old days*, he thought. He did not have to wait long before two men entered and stood in front of him.

"Major Stanek, my name is Gregory Smith, and this is Sam Long," he said pointing to the other, younger man. Charlie quickly sized them up. Smith was older and heavier, with greying hair. He looked to be trim and fit. The other was much younger, shorter, yet looked fit. Both men wore dark suits, and Charlie thought, had rather plain looking faces.

"We've been tasked the job of debriefing you on your recent assignment to South Vietnam.," he said. Both men sat across from Charlie. "I hope you had a good trip. Quite long, eh?" He tried to smile.

Charlie stared at him. "Damn long and I'm tired so get on with it."

Long opened the folder and removed a tablet, and with a pen prepared to write. The interview began. The hours passed. Long took copious notes rapidly as they spoke. He never asked to repeat or slow down.

Charlie told them everything from his initial contact with Stover and Jon Grey, but omitting his contacts with the Viet

Minh. Through the hours, Smith never once asked about Jack's death, which surprised Charlie.

"I get the solid impression from you that our current policy to support the Diem government is folly. Even with his recent victories against domestic enemies. Do I have that right, Major?" Smith asked as if a concluding remark was necessary.

"That is my impression, yes, from what I observed," Charlie replied, growing tired and restless. These two were born to do this, he thought, staring up at the ceiling. And they are damn good at it.

"I think you've given us your reason," Smith said. "Sam read it back."

He read every page of notes back to them, almost verbatim. "Is that accurate, sir?" he then asked Charlie.

"As far as I can tell, yes," Charlie replied. "But I would like to know about John Sawyer's murder. Can you share any information?"

"Yes well, you know his real identity then?"

"Of course," he said. Not bothering to mention he had searched his room. "Who poisoned him and why? Can you help me with that?"

"Sorry, but we can't help you," he said flatly. "Sam, type everything up and get it ready for the briefing." He turned to his accomplice.

"Right away," Sam replied, standing. "Major," he nodded to Charlie, and then turned with papers in hand to leave.

"Major, tomorrow morning you will be brought here for another meeting," Smith said, standing. "Perhaps then, you will get your questions answered and have a better understanding of the situation."

Charlie watched him silently.

"We have found you suitable quarters and your driver will take you. Good day." He prepared to leave, and then quickly turned back to Charlie. "Oh yeah, I must add, Major, I am familiar with your exploits on behalf of the United States. Quite a hero," he said, then again turned to leave the room.

Charlie waited sullenly for the driver. Nothing has changed, he thought, only the faces.

He was hoping for more luxurious accommodations. He looked around the room, and was disappointed at what he saw. Left over from the war, he decided, sitting on the soft bed. World War 2. He wondered if they had him under surveillance, bugged the room. He searched but found nothing. Later in the evening, he decided a drink was in order.

He located a corner tap near his quarters, walked in and nestled up to the mahogany bar. "Bourbon," he called to the bartender. "The best you got."

The bartender, an older man with blue eyes and no hair anywhere on his head, Charlie noticed, poured the drink in front of him.

He quickly drained it and ordered another.

"Hard day?" a well-dressed man said, sitting next to him.

"Hard enough," Charlie replied, content to sip the second Bourbon. He did not bother to look at the man. He had had enough of the day and had no interest in engaging this guy in conversation.

"I bet you're dealing with the bureaucracy around here. You look tired and frustrated." He moved to a stool next to Charlie.

"A long flight."

"From?"

"Southeast Asia," Charlie replied, providing the man with a vague but honest answer.

"You in the army?" the man asked. "By the way, my name is John Sitter."

"John, I'm Charlie." They shook hands. "No, to answer your question. I'm a contractor."

"I know all about contracting with Uncle Sam. What kind?"

"I give advice mostly, but no one seems to listen," Charlie said. "How about you?"

"I work for the Eisenhower Administration."

"Good for you," Charlie finished his drink and ordered a third. The booze was going down easy, relaxing him.

"I organize arms shipments to Chiang's boys. At the Pentagon."

"Who?"

"You know...Chiang Kai shek, the President of Free China.

"I think you're too late," Charlie replied, offering more than a hint of sarcasm.

"John laughed. "Not really. Big military build -up for when Mao invades the island."

"Is that a priority, what with Europe and the Russians?"

"Sure is," John said, surprised at the question. "Mao has close to three quarter million Commies there. We got to get ready for the big fight."

"Are you worried about Indochina?"

"Yup," John replied. "That's the next domino to fall, so we're preparing to build up forces there, too."

"Good luck." Charlie said it flatly so he would not upset John.

"Guns and bullets, eh?" he laughed again.

"Don't forget airplanes, jets, too."

He looked at Charlie, not knowing if it was cynicism or unsolicited advice. "Airplanes, too."

"The world is going to hell, ain't it?" Charlie said. He paid his tab, and left. I got to focus on 1,000 head of sheep, he told himself, strolling back to the hotel. And getting back to my kid.

The next morning bright and early, the same driver escorted Charlie back to the same building, then into the same room. He waited. Within minutes, two different men entered and sat down. "I'm Joseph Ling, and he is James Bright, and as you've probably figured, we are from the Directorate of Operations upstairs.

The speaker, Charlie figured the most senior and would probably do all the talking. He began by opening a file he had carried in with him. "Major, I must caution you, everything we discuss in this room is "Top Secret," involving highly classified information."

"I understand," Charlie said.

"How well did you know John Sawyer?" he began.

"Not well. We met only a couple of days before traveling to Saigon."

"Later?"

"I gradually learned he had his own mission in Vietnam. I realized this by observing his actions there. He never shared much of what that mission was. I suspected he was advising the National Army on building an intelligence section," Charlie explained. "He did tell me he spoke fluent Chinese but no Vietnamese."

"You are correct, Major," Ling said. "That was only part of his assignment there.

"The other?"

"We brought him in to neutralize the Viet Minh leadership which you would reveal through your discussions with Madame Thieu. That didn't happen so through intelligence gathering he had to locate them himself."

"To kill them."

He ignored the comment. "We believed and still believe that the success of the Diem government hinges on neutralizing the procommunist forces still in the South."

"His mission?"

"Yes, does that surprise you?"

"Not really, but..." He shrugged. "Jack, the name given to me, never seemed that comfortable with the people or the setting."

The two agents looked at each other. "He was our man in China, doing various things for the U.S. Government. His effectiveness was limited but he was successful overall."

Bright handed Ling another file. He took it and quickly reviewed the documents inside while Charlie sat, growing increasingly impatient.

"Your record is impressive, Major. Your success for us in clandestine operations in both Southeast Asia and in Central Europe is outstanding." He continued reading the dossier. "Hmm, then you suddenly disappeared in 1946. We located you in Australia. The notation states that your activities after your work in Central Europe were monitored but we chose not to intervene."

"You boys seem to know everything about my life."

"They both smiled. "Of course, Major." He continued perusing the dossier. "I think your greatest achievement was exposing and terminating Attila. Most impressive."

"I had help," Charlie said. "Get to the point."

"We need you."

"What?"

"Here's the situation confronting us. We have only recently learned that the Chinese Ministry of Public Security is actively working worldwide against our allies and us probably with assistance from the Russians. Ho Chi Minh's government in the North is also involved in espionage activities. Both are working in the South, according to our sources. We believe, and have evidence to support our beliefs, that one of their agents ordered John Sawyer killed."

"Why?"

"Sawyer, as it turns out, was known to them. They learned that he was involved in activities in China that cost the lives of several high officials in CCP's intelligence service. The Chinese discovered, according to our sources, that he was in Saigon tracking high ranking Viet Minh cadre in the South."

"They determined to kill him?" Charlie asked. "What about the KGB. I would think they would be somehow involved. They are supplying Ho Chi Minh with arms like the Chinese, are they not?"

"Yes, but..." Ling looked to his partner. Charlie knew they were deciding how much to reveal. "There are Russians in Saigon. We know this, but after Stalin's death in '53 and the internal struggle in the Kremlin to succeed him, we believe the KGB slowed or even curtailed espionage operations in that part of the world."

"But you don't really know, do you?"

"Let's get back to Chinese interference in Indochina." Ling said, ignoring Charlie's question. "They want to bring the Vietnamese into their orbit, shall we say, and our goal, of course, is to prevent it."

"I've been told the Vietnamese hate the Chinese. Ancient enemies. The expression is 'once the Chinese come they never leave.' I was told that. You know...unwelcome house guests and all that."

"They're all Commies. That's bad enough." Ling said.

"I don't know how I can assist. I speak not a word of Chinese or Vietnamese.

"That's not necessary."

"Why?"

"We think the hit on Sawyer was ordered out of Europe."

"Where?"

"London, Paris, or Berlin, we think."

"It's a small world, isn't it?"

"Very, I fear," Ling replied. He watched Charlie closely. "We want you to find the agent and the assassin."

"You're asking me then to expose a Communist spy ring, aren't you?"

"No, the Ministry of Public Security is already too large to destroy, with agents in Asia, Europe, and the United States. We want you to find the agent responsible for killing Sawyer," he said. "This is critical to national security and we must demonstrate we know what kind of activities they're engaged in."

"Revenge, eh?" Charlie said.

Ling frowned, not wanting to hear that. "The U.S. is dealing with major issues in Asia as well as in Europe. The power of the Chinese Communists is growing. They are an expansionist power. Soon Taiwan and Indochina. They're hurting us, and we must limit their espionage capabilities."

"I see. What about the Russians?"

"We don't know if they have agents on the ground in Saigon."

"I can tell you they do," Charlie said. "I get this from a Viet Minh friendly source."

Smith wrote that down but neither man responded to Charlie's accusation.

"You're our man, who we can drop on the ground immediately. You are an unknown quantity to the Chinese, and you operate alone. Perfect for the job."

"I'm well-known to the KGB. What if they learn I'm in Europe?"

Ling smiled an all-knowing smile. "The cold war world has moved on from your adventures of seven years ago. I think you're completely off their radar."

Charlie was not buying any of it, but chose to say nothing. "I'll need support and contacts in Europe."

"We have someone there to greet and brief you. I think you know him."

"Who would that be?" he asked curious.

"Henry Eisenberg. Know him?"

Charlie smiled. "Well, that was a few years ago." They were throwing him back into Cold War action and it was happening so fast Charlie felt in a daze. He forced himself to consider options if he declined their request: *as vindictive as I know them to be, they could prevent me from returning to the Outback. What then? The world has shrunk and hiding from them is far more difficult*, he decided.

"When do I leave?" He gave in and immediately regretted it.

The two agents smiled. "When this mission is completed, you can return to Australia no longer bothered by us. I promise you."

Both men watched Charlie. He seemed unmoved, his brows furled. He had 'no deal' written all over his face. Ling immediately saw that it was not enough of an offer. "I will personally ensure you are granted citizenship there," Ling said.

"That's a deal." Charlie quickly agreed. They shook on it, but he was skeptical, remembering the earlier deal in Canberra.

Chapter 22

Charlie really did not know how to get out of this job. *I cannot disappear again with a young child to look after, and saying no does not appear to work. The bastards are so damn persuasive,* he thought.

The flight to London was peaceful. He still had no idea how to begin the assignment, but knew the way forward would gradually reveal itself. It always did. He flew this time as a TWA passenger and civilian air transportation was pleasant and comfortable, he decided.

Henry, he thought about the small man who smuggled Jews out of Europe and worked with American intelligence after the war. *He knows I cannot cross over—far too dangerous. I am still certain the Russians and the Czechs remember me despite what Ling said, so I stay in the West. That narrows things a bit, and reduces the threat level for me. Rosebud, she could be helpful. Charlie thought about Marie in deep cover in Prague. Espionage, what a dirty game.*

He saw Henry immediately after passing through Customs with his single suitcase. A small man, dark hair, dark eyes, dark suit. So appropriate, Charlie thought. Henry waited, almost invisible in the small crowd waiting to meet passengers.

The passport they gave Charlie said "Charles Lee Klinehoff." He traveled as an American tourist returning to the Old Country to visit relatives. He liked the name for some reason.

"Charles, we meet again," Henry said, extending his hand.

"Henry, I never thought I would see you again. The last we were together you were going to settle permanently in Israel. What happened?"

"Too unsettled there, always a war," he replied, "and I ran out of money. An old man needs money to live comfortably so I go back to work."

"I understand."

"Yes, and London is comfortable for me. I am alone now. My wife died after I last saw you." They strolled through the concourse, neither in much of a hurry.

"I lost my wife, too. It was difficult, Henry, very difficult for me...and my son."

"You have a son, eh? That is good, I think," he said, smiling. "They are the best hope for us."

"I wonder." Charlie also smiled sadly, a bitter, sweet smile.

"You are the best there is, my friend." Henry patted him on the back. "You are trying to make the world right."

From Heathrow, they took a train into London. The two old friends took the time to catch up on each other's world. Charlie quickly saw that it took him far less time to describe life as an operator of a sheep station in Southcentral Australia. For Henry, the story was much longer. He talked of life in the Middle East, wars with the Muslim countries, changes in Europe since '48, and finally, his life in England. "I like it here. My neighbors are people from all over the world. They avoided the task at hand— the elephant in the room.

Henry lived in a small flat on the East End. Looking around the neighborhood, Charlie saw the mix he spoke of—

racial and religious diversity. His flat with two bedrooms, nicely but simply furnished, with few wall hangings or other personal things. He suspected that highlighted Henry's life. But Charlie understood.

After a meal prepared by Henry, they focused on serious business. "Asians are here in London, too, but the emigre community is much larger in Paris, and more open to intrigue. Go there," he said.

"I would think a large Indochinese community as well."

"Yes. You will make contact with a Chinese emigre working with American intelligence when you arrive. His name is Jack Liu Quan. Here is his address. Memorize it and then destroy it. He is a shopkeeper—Chinese antiquities-- who knows his community. He will tell you who supports Ho Chi Minh. A very resourceful man, I think."

"Are American agents operating near?"

"Probably not," Henry replied, and continued. "Russian agents are never far away, Be very careful. Someone may remember you as the man who killed General Andre Pavlov. Too capture or kill you would be quite a coup for that person."

"They told me in Washington that the struggle for power in the Kremlin has disrupted their espionage activities. What do you think about that, Henry?"

"Ha!" he quipped. "Perhaps some disruption, but I think their operations have not been compromised in the least."

He watched Henry stand to walk into a bedroom. When he returned, he carried an object wrapped in an oily cloth.

"Here, take this. You may need it," Henry said, handing Charlie the object.

Charlie unfolded the cloth. He looked at a small .32 caliber Colt pocket automatic.

"A good weapon for you, I think."

"I appreciate the gift."

"I get from an Englishman, not a Webley," Henry said. "Hide it in your suitcase." He then handed Charlie several tickets. "Take the train to the Channel. After you cross, take this train to Paris. I made Hotel reservations in the name of Charles Klinehoff at the Rochambeau Hotel. It is comfortable but not luxurious, and in the section of the city where many Asians live including Vietnamese."

Charlie examined each ticket.

"You are a tourist at all time. Henry handed him a camera, and pair of sunglasses. "Your disguise, eh?" He smiled.

Charlie tried the glasses on. *Nice look*, he decided.

"One more thing. No one knows of your arrival, not even the Americans. When you meet Mr. Quan, give the password. "Freedom. He will reply, "Independence.""

"Freedom, independence," Charlie repeated.

"A word of caution, my friend. Your assignment is only to identify the responsible agent, and always keep an eye out for the Russians. They are always watching. But do not shoot him if you find him." He smiled. "For us, those days are over, we hope. I give you my gun only for your protection," Henry said. "Find him and leave France. Return here."

"I understand." Charlie felt relieved.

"Remember, you are an American tourist like thousands of others, who travel to Paris in the summertime, so see the sights. Enjoy your visit."

He thought Henry was overdoing the tourist routine a bit. No clandestine work I was ever involved in was very pleasant without a worry that someone may shoot me, except my nights in Saigon with Truin.

Charlie and Henry said their good byes and he was on his way. The Channel crossing was a little rough for him, but he very much enjoyed the train trips through the English and French countrysides. The world seemed so idyllic and peaceful. One almost forgets that a short ten or twelve years earlier the region was ripped apart by world war, he thought. He saw sheep grazing in the fenced-in pastures, comparing the view with the vast spaces of Australia.

He had never been to Paris, but like most, had heard so much about "the city of light." Looking forward to his stay, he decided he had at least to see the more famous sites such as the Louvre, Eiffel Tower, and visit several of the more famous neighborhoods while in town.

The train whistled that it was entering a terminal. By the time it had jerked to a stop, Charlie stood by the door prepared to disembark. With suitcase in-hand, he walked slowly through the large Victorian-style building, navigating the crowds of people. He began to feel he was blending into the Parisian post war world. He was excited, and for the moment, shoved aside thoughts of his mission to find a dangerous spy with connections to the Indochinese.

He walked the city, stopping occasionally to find his way and stop at an outdoor café for a coffee and pastry. He was reminded of his first meeting with Marta at an outdoor café in Prague. That seemed like so long ago.

He bought a map in a small bookshop called Shakespeare's he discovered along the Seine near Notre Dame. He searched out the Hotel Rochambeau. Their subway still under construction, he took a bus for the remainder of his journey.

The hotel had his reservation. He presented his passport to the clerk, a small dapper man with a beaming smile. ""Mr. Klinehoff," he read. "German?" The man spoke good English.

"The name is, yes."

An older woman showed him to his room on the top floor of the five-story hotel. She spoke passable English. He asked her if she was familiar with Quan's Antique Shop. "I'm looking for a small piece for my wife and was referred to Quan's," he told her.

"I do not know it, monsieur," she answered. "But I may know the street where it is located, in Chinatown. Look there and good luck. They are close to the hotel."

He departed the hotel and began to walk. He decided the best place to carry the automatic was tucked into his belt in the small of his back.

Strolling the area, Charlie, consulting his map, learned that two neighborhoods—Place Maubert and Marne – la- Vallee—was where the Indochinese community mostly lived. Within a short distance of several blocks, he began to see more and more mostly Vietnamese restaurants and cafes. He chose a small café in an ancient building in the middle of the block. He entered, seating himself. Quickly perusing the menu, he ordered a bowl of Pho with pork. The waiter was a young man.

Charlie engaged him in casual conversation while eating. He discovered the young man was Vietnamese. Despite his limited English, he explained his father owned the café.

"Where did you learn to speak English?" Charlie asked. "You speak well."

"From GIs who come to Paris, He said, proud of the complement. "I born here and very young during the occupation and war with the Nazis."

"I, too, was an American soldier who fought against the Nazis," Charlie replied. "Now, I am a tourist visiting the sites."

The young man appeared interested in the conversation, pumping Charlie for more information on that war. Charlie was the only customer so he sat at the table across from him, leisurely spending his time.

"I want to purchase a small piece of jewelry for my wife. Can you recommend a shop?"

"Oui, monsieur," the young man said, happy to assist. He directed him to a shop near the café. "My friend work in Nguyen's Jewelry and Antiques. You go there and say Ngo Nhieu sent you, He give you good deal."

Charlie easily found the street. He walked down both sides, casually looking in shop windows and through vendor stalls.

He saw Nguyen's shop, examined merchandize displayed, and then moved on. Finally, after strolling both sides of the street, he found Quan's Rare Antiques and Imports. He entered.

The room was very narrow but filled with items from floor to ceiling. He saw jewelry, small porcelain objects, and carved jade pieces under the counter. Shelves lined the walls with everything from jars with pickled snakes inside, brightly painted vases, to daggers, short swords, even a musket. He saw several watercolors on the floor in a corner.

An older man greeted him, stepping from a back room. "May I help you?" he asked politely with patience." What do you look for?" the man asked. He had a soft voice and peaceful green eyes.

"Mr. Quan?" Charlie asked. There was no one else in the small shop.

"I am Jack Quan," he answered. "Do I know you, sir?"

"No. I have been sent to you."

Quan said nothing as a reply. "You are English or American?" he finally asked.

"American," Charlie replied. "Freedom."

The man nodded. "Independence. Come." Quan went to lock his door then returned.

Charlie followed him into the back room. He must live here, Charlie observed. Here the walls were lined with books, stacks of magazines, some in English, some in Chinese, covered the floor.

Quan motioned for him to sit. He quickly looked at the front room and through the window. *A very thorough yet nervous man*, Charlie thought, watching him.

"I get tea." Soon, he returned from another even smaller room with a porcelain teapot and cups. He set the pot down and offered Charlie a cup. "Now, how I can I assist you, mister, mister?"

"Klinehoff, Charles Klinehoff," he replied.

"Yes, Klinehoff," Quan repeated slowly. He waited patiently for Charlie to continue.

"I'm looking for a man, perhaps Chinese, who ordered a hit on an American agent in Saigon. Poison."

What kind?"

"Arsenic."

"Now there are better, quicker methods to kill someone," Quan replied. "Are you certain he was Chinese?"

"I was told he was," Charlie replied. "The dead agent had worked in China, mainland, too. He may have had enemies there."

"Who wish him dead...," he said. "Where was he killed?"

"In Saigon."

"Saigon? How strange." Quan took his time, considering the information Charlie provided. "Chinese Communist agents come and go through Paris. The French Republic is open, chaotic. A perfect place to conduct business. With many French Communists, it is not inhospitable to Chinese, Russians, and especially Indochinese."

"I've been told this."

"I suspect the North may have been involved in this assassination. Have you considered this?"

"I have, but my superiors insist on believing Mao's government is involved."

"Of course. The Vietnamese spy network is very young and crude. They often must rely on Chinese and Russians for intelligence," Quan said. To Charlie, he sounded very knowledgeable on the subject. "The Chinese are professionals, in operation since the 1920s, but Ho Chi Minh's network is only a few years old, and must depend on amateurs to do their dirty work. The American agent...why was he in Saigon?"

"He was working with the National Army helping to build a counter-espionage unit."

Quan listened and nodded slightly. "I think he was there to do much more, Mr. Klinehoff. To kill someone, perhaps, eh?"

"Probably," Charlie replied.

"Hmm, I think not one of Zhao's boys. They not interested in Vietnam, and too dangerous to involve themselves. Vietnamese make too many mistakes. I think the North ordered it."

This man's insights impressed Charlie. *This puts a completely different spin on Jack's death,* he thought, *if he is correct.*

"Would they order a hit from Paris? That seems convoluted to me."

Quan shrugged. "I don't know. If money is involved, perhaps. Remember Vietnamese Communists are here, too."

"Any names?"

"With so many new arrivals to Paris from North Africa and Asia, I know little. I think one man to watch is Quac Tan, son of General Duc , Diem's top general. He is, how you say, a playboy, and always need money. His father no give him."

Vouc's fiancé, Charlie knew already. "Interesting. Where can I find him?"

"He likes to go to fine hotels in Paris. He is friends with many Russians. Paris has many, mostly aristocrats who come after revolution and Stalin's purges."

"Any Russians who support Moscow? KGB?"

"Probably," he replied. "They frequent France, I think."

"What about emigres who live in Paris?"

"Many people have relatives still in Russia, so they are forced to accommodate the Kremlin in many ways. Assistance? Money, maybe?"

"Names?"

"No names, but the emigres hang out at a large cafe called Bistro du Romanov," Quan said. "Appropriate, yes?"

"Mr. Quan, you've been most helpful." He got up to leave.

"One more thing, Mr. Klinehoff."

"Yes?"

"If KGB, beware," Quan said ominously. "They probably already know of your arrival and are watching us. They miss nothing."

"Thanks for your help." He turned and marched for the door with Jack Quan watching from the back room.

Bistro du Romanov, a good place to begin, he decided, walking into groups of shoppers congregating along the street. Charlie happened to notice a European-looking man standing near a vegetable cart, only steps from the shop. He was dressed in a shabby suit, clean-shaven, and hatless with black hair combed back.

Charlie continued walking, but not back to his hotel. Turning into a crowded side street, he stopped and waited. Just a hunch, he thought.

Soon the man crossed the narrow street. Charlie followed him at a safe distance. After several blocks, the man stopped to hail a cab. The vehicle sped away.

Charlie also stopped a cab. "Bistro du Romanov," he ordered. "Do you know it?"

"Oui," the driver nodded.

The ride was short. Charlie exited the cab, paid the driver, and crossed the street. He casually walked by the café several times before entering. He found an empty table along a wall near the window and sat.

A young woman approached, handing him a menu. He ordered in Russian, a language he spoke fluently, but hesitantly as he had not spoken it in seven years.

The young woman did not understand him very well. She looked at him perplexed.

"No Russian?" he asked her in English.

"No, I only work here," she replied in very good English. "I am a student at the American University."

Charlie explained he was an English tourist and seeing Paris for the first time. He asked if she could recommend a guide for several days.

"I think you are American," she replied with a smile. "I can show you the sights, monsieur."

"What's your name?" he asked. Charlie guessed her to be early twenties, and very pretty. Her long dark hair rolled into a bun, but he found her large green eyes beguiling. They seemed to draw him in. Thinking she an employee not directly associated with the patrons, he hoped to get information from her, but mostly, he just wanted to chat with someone.

"Juliet, monsieur."

He ordered, and when she departed, he scanned the café, trying to get a sense of the place and who frequented it. A mostly older and female crowd, he saw.

Juliet quickly returned with his order, smiling as she set the plate down. She poured his wine.

An interesting smile, he decided and tried to make conversation while she poured the wine.

"The best for Americans," she offered, smiling. She turned to another customer, wine in hand.

"Merci," he said, watching her. He liked the sway of her hips under the short skirt.

As he took his first bite of bread and cheese, a man entered who he recognized. Charlie watched him enter and sit opposite from him across the room. He followed me, Charlie observed, watching his movements from the corner of his eye. The man sat, and promptly Juliet approached him to take his order. He considered whether the man picked him up at Quan's shop or if he tracked him from the hotel.

Chapter 23

Charlie learned nothing at the bistro other than he was tailed by a Russian. The young woman offered little in the way of intelligence. *I must somehow learn who he works for,* he decided, with options flying at him, *and I must assume he knows where I stay.*

His only accomplishment in the bistro was hiring Juliet to take him sightseeing in the morning. He also hoped she would be more forthcoming in divulging information about the bistro's Russian patrons if away from her place of employment. They would meet in the hotel lobby.

He waited until darkness had descended on the city, checked his automatic, and left his room for the lobby. The lobby was empty of people and the clerk looked asleep sitting behind the high desk. *I'll walk,* he decided, leaving the hotel. Following the same route he took earlier, he walked by Quan's shop. He saw the "closed" sign on the door. The place was dark—front and back. He checked the door. Not locked so he entered, slowly and carefully. He pulled the automatic from the small of his back. "Mr. Quan," he called. "Jack Quan."

No reply. He entered the back room and looked around. Quan was not there either. He turned on the lamp light and searched the place. The arrangement of items in the back, private rooms of Quan seemed different, moved around haphazardly. Under the chair where he sat earlier, he saw the teapot. It was shattered.

He returned to the front of the shop, turned on the light, then returned to the rear, sitting where Quan sat earlier. He turned off the rear light and sat in the darkness. He watched the front, automatic resting in his lap. He hoped either Quan or an intruder would return soon.

An hour passed, then two. He was preparing to stand and leave when the door opened. A man entered and closed the door without uttering a word. Someone had muffled the doorbell earlier.

When the intruder had walked to the middle of the shop room, Charlie announced his presence, pointing the .32 at the man. He immediately recognized the man as his tail.

Charlie immediately flipped the light switch, startling the intruder. "Stop," he ordered in English. The man looked at him not understanding. He repeated it in Russian. The man understood.

Charlie was quickly in his face. Holding the .32 at the man's head, he began to thoroughly search him. The man was not armed. Charlie retrieved a wallet and nothing else. "Come with me," he said in Russian, forcing the man into the back at gunpoint.

"Sit down." Charlie quickly leafed through the wallet searching for an ID. His passport—Russian.

"Yuri, start talking or you're a dead man.

The man grunted without a word spoken.

Charlie backhanded him across the face. "Manners, asshole," he said in Russian. "KGB bastard?" He backhanded him again.

Blood began to flow from the man's broad nose. His dark eyes blurred. He shook his head to try to regain his composure. "American prick," he growled, barely audible.

"Where is Jack Quan, KGB stoolie?"

At first, Yuri did not respond. "He ok, no worry," he finally mumbled in heavily accented English. Blood dripped onto his white shirt.

"Liar," Charlie said, pressing the .32 harder into the man's temple.

"No, Quan ok," he mumbled.

Charlie pointed the automatic at Yuri's knee, and clicked off the safety. I've learned many things from KGB," he said. "First, I shoot you in the right kneecap, then the left, until you scream in pain. If you do not talk, I kill you. Simple plan, eh Yuri?"

He spit at Charlie. "Ha! American, no guts," he said bravely or foolishly.

Charlie fired. The man screamed. It was only a grazing wound but Yuri did not know that yet. "Now the other." He pointed the pistol to the other knee.

"KGB know about you, Charles Stanek. They want you."

"How?"

"They follow you from America."

"They? Who do you work for?" Charlie said. "Give me answers and you may live, Yuri."

"Not KGB," he said finally. "Poor Russian emigre, not KGB."

"Who?" Charlie repeated.

The man was silent.

"Tell me or I can make this very, very painful for you. What will it be?"

"No KGB. I work for Madame Kershef. She pay me to follow you. Follow you only, not kill. I, a very poor man with four babies to feed."

"Where is this Madame Kershef?"

Charlie scouted the second story flat located in a very prosperous neighborhood of Paris before he entered. Yuri's description of her was that she was old and very rich, a Russian aristocrat who settled in Paris in the 1920's. She grew wealthy by selling her services to Bolsheviks and the English intelligence service, whoever paid more.

He left the Russian tied up in Quan's back room. He stopped the nose bleeding and wrapped a rag around the knee, figuring it would keep him, at least until he took care of his business.

He saw that she lived alone, no bodyguards he could locate, with a light security system, not even a concierge. He knocked on her door.

The old woman answered after only several knocks. "Oui?" she asked.

"Yuri," he replied with his best Russian accent. "Let me in."

She let him in immediately.

Charlie immediately pointed the gun in her face. "Madame Kershef, we talk," he said in Russian. The woman's flaming red hair, as thin as it was with grey roots pulled back tightly. Her eyes seemed alive...with venom. Bitterness, anger, Charlie could not tell, but the lines and scars on her face and neck screamed out at him. Yup, he decided standing there, one hard bitch.

She stepped back to allow him entrance. She seemed unafraid of him. Her blue eyes burned. "Who are you to invade my home? A bandit?"

"Charles Stanek," he said.

The burning eyes immediately turned to surprise, then quickly to interest.

"Sit down, old woman," he ordered.

She did.

A quick observation told him the flat was richly furnished. He saw photos on every table—young, old people but none of Lenin or Nickolas II.

"You're too old for a KGB whore. Why do you follow me?"

She looked at him with contempt. "You...Stanek. I've wanted to meet you, but no, I'm a private contractor not KGB," she said. "I'm a capitalist. I work for money not useless ideas and dreams of tomorrow."

"Who hired you to follow me?"

"I can't tell you my secrets, Mr. Stanek. Then no one would hire me."

"How long have you been following me? Since London?"

She smiled. "It seems you are a man who is very hard to kill. In Saigon, they tried to get Vietnamese to do it, but they failed miserably. They believed they had lost you." She smiled again. "Then suddenly you appear in London. Oh yes, the KGB knows about the old man, Henry Weisenberg. The KGB always watches him these days, but we were surprised to see you there. Yes, your photo is everywhere, such a famous man you are."

Charlie listened, his fear and anxiety growing.

"In Saigon, an agent saw you, recognized you. You were everywhere, so easy to follow, yet, it seems, so well protected. You have a lover there, eh? Your Viet Minh protector?"

"What do you want from me?"

She sighed. "Tell me of the American deep agent in Czechoslovakia. Ahh, Rosebud, she is called. I could get millions of rubles for that bit of information. I'd even split it with you."

"Go to hell. Never."

"We suspected as much," she replied, shaking her head. "That makes things much more difficult for you. If they cannot make you talk, the KGB will kill you. Perhaps, they will just kill you, anyway. Too bad. You are a handsome man. A family?"

"Go to hell." He repeated it, this time with more anger.

"The KGB will find you. Then what, Mr. Stanek?"

"What if I shoot you now?" He began to understand she knew nothing of Jack's murder, nor did she probably care.

"It won't matter. Someone else will do my work. Many hungry people in our troubled world. Men like Yuri, who I suspect you have already met. I do hope you did not hurt him too much."

"You are unscrupulous."

"Yes, I don't really care which side pays me, but I do know that long after their vicious game is played out, we the survivors will still be around."

Charlie lowered his weapon.

"My work is over. The KGB paid me handsomely to find you and follow you. I have done that. Now it is up to them, Mr. Stanek."

"I should kill you now and save the world from your evil."

"But you won't. You won't because you are a man of honor. Too bad," she said, watching him, looking into his eyes, face, everything about him scrutinized.

He easily felt her eyes.

"Give me a name so I can at least defend myself."

"They are a nameless, faceless bunch—men in grey suits like the Americans and British," she said. "Good luck to you, Mr. Charles Stanek. And a bit of advice. Never come to Europe again or you risk death at the hands of the KGB. Stay in America or Asia where they must rely on informants, an untrustworthy lot, it seems."

"Thanks for the advice."

"I tell you these things, Mr. Stanek, because I like you. Now go away, and quickly."

Charlie left the way he had come. He returned to his room but could not, would not sleep. *What have I learned?* he asked himself as he paced about the room. *Vietnamese murdered Jack?*

The hours ticked away. Sleep was impossible. He held his weapon close.

The next morning he prepared his escape. He was now appreciating the CIA's deep pockets as he had money, and lots of it to get back to Asia. *Alone without contacts*, he thought sadly, and quickly finished dressing. And not even Henry to help.

He left his suitcase in the room and took the stairs to the lobby and outside. He looked around for Juliet, did not see her. He hoped to see her one last time before he disappeared.

A honk. Charlie looked. Off on a side street he saw an ancient Citroen and a young woman waving to him.

Carefully scanning the street to ensure they were not watching him, he ran to the car.

He did not notice but a man, not Yuri, watched him from inside a nearby café. The man smiled an evil smile, knowing he had IDed Charlie.

Chapter 24

The first stop on the tour was Versailles. He had read much about the 18th Century palace and grounds with its 1919 significance in its Hall of Mirrors.

It's outside the city. We'll have to drive a few minutes to get there," Juliet said, shifting the old car into gear. Charlie thought he heard clanging, becoming especially noisy at higher speeds.

"Juliet, don't take the direct route," he said, looking behind them at traffic.

She looked with surprise and fear at him. "Why Charlie? There's a problem?

"Just being cautious," he lied.

And she knew he was lying. "You Americans...too many gangster movies."

"I guess you're right." They both laughed, each masking its seriousness.

On the royal grounds, they walked looking and talking, and growing more comfortable with each other. Soon, they were much more than working acquaintances.

He caught her watching him when he took the time to examine small items of interest to him. "What?" he asked, feeling her eyes on him.

"You remind me of a friend, a lover who one day disappeared to leave me in Paris penniless. Where I never knew, maybe he is traveling, or the French Foreign Legion off fighting in Africa or in Indochina." She smiled at him sadly but warmly. She softly touched his hand.

The remainder of the day unfolded in a similar manner. Charlie told her of his new life in Australia on a sheep ranch. He spoke of his lost wife and young son who waited for him. His openness surprised even him. Juliet appeared most interested in Australia, so he described all the places he had visited there.

"Your work brings you to Paris. How strange, she said while they took a coffee break on their return to the city. "Does a sheep man have enemies so far from home?"

He looked at her, the beautiful face beaming with curiosity. "I have other work that is much more dangerous. Please do not ask what, and I say this to protect you."

"Charlie, man of mystery," she said and held his arm tightly.

He sipped his coffee. "I have one final request from you after such a wonderful day spent seeing Paris with a beautiful young Parisian."

"Yes?" she asked blushing, again not knowing if he was serious. "What is it, Monsieur Charlie?"

"When darkness comes, I want you to drop me at a very congested corner near the train station. Then you must forget you ever knew me."

Juliet looked at him shocked. "Charlie?"

"Please, take this money, and do as I ask." He handed her French Franks, and then prepared for a quick exit as they neared the train station. Pausing suddenly, he leaned over in the narrow sedan and kissed Juliet on the cheek. "You have given me a wonderful day that I will never forget," he said. "Thank you."

"Oh Charlie," She reached over to grab his arm. "Wait!"

"I must get out of Paris."

"I have a better idea." She pulled away from the curb.

"Where are we going?"

"First to my room for a passport, then to Switzerland. I will drive you." She accelerated, and the old car raced into traffic.

She drove the Citroen like a pro. Charlie held on.

Juliet was fast, returning within minutes with a small bag. She now wore her beret that made Charlie smile. *So idealistic and she doesn't even know if I'm one of the good guys.*

She got in, threw her bag in the rear and they roared off. "We must stop for petrol, she said. "Then east to the Swiss border." She was visibly excited.

"Juliet, you are placing your life in grave danger by helping me," he said, wanting to give her another opportunity to get away from him. "You know nothing about me. I could be KGB, an assassin, anyone."

"Never, Charlie. I know what I feel," she said, shifting and navigating through traffic. "You are alone...like me. We will get through this together."

I can't use her and risk her life. No good, he thought, torn. "We run from the KGB and they are a murderous lot. Do you understand that?"

"Please Charlie. I am a grown woman who makes her own decisions."

"They could be following us now. They seem to have eyes everywhere and they want me real bad."

"What did you do to them?"

"I have information they urgently want. But, I think, most importantly, it is about revenge." Charlie heard the clanging again and decided it was the transmission. "Do you think your car will make it to the border?"

"Of course, Charles Klinehoff. Have faith."

"Oh, another thing. The name is Charles Stanek. You should know it. Everyone else in Europe appears to know it."

"Charles Stanek," she repeated it. "Czech?"

"Yes, my family came from near Prague to Wisconsin about 50 years ago."

"Was your farm in Australia a lie?"

"It's a station. No, that's the truth. I moved there after the war," he said.

"You must take me there. I must see this station, Charles Stanek."

He smiled. "Your family—mother, father?"

The Nazis killed my father during the war. He fought in the resistance. My mother..."

Charlie saw the tears form in her eyes.

"My mother died two years ago. She was not well."

"Brothers and sisters?"

"No one." They were leaving the metropolitan area. Juliet pulled her skirt to her thighs to drive more comfortably.

"I'm sorry," Charlie replied. "Two people alone in an angry world, eh Juliet." He smiled softly, more for her sake. "But we will succeed. I know this."

"How old are you, Charlie? You seem too young to have such powerful enemies."

He laughed. "It would seem. I am 36. You?"

"A woman should never tell her age, Charles Stanek, but I will tell you. I am 22."

"Your studies? Were they getting boring for you?"

"I lied to you. I dropped out of university two years ago when my mama died."

"Too bad, an education is very important."

She smiled. "You talk like a father."

"I am."

Have you ever gone to university?"

"I graduated from the University of Chicago."

Neither spoke again until darkness began to set in. Charlie closed his eyes to consider a plan to get out of Europe. He knew that once in Switzerland, it was very difficult to get out. He wondered how to get rid of Juliet safely. *Such a foolish but adventurous young woman,* he thought with a smile. Nearing the border much later in the evening, Charlie decided he had to talk with her.

"Juliet, we cannot cross the border here. I would not be able to get out for weeks, maybe months due to circumstances. I want you to drop me off at the nearest rural train station, then return to Paris."

"No," she said simply.

"You are a very stubborn young woman," he said. "I must tell you how the KGB gathers information from its captives. They use torture then they kill you. I do not want that for you."

"Too late. I have made my decision.

"Which is?"

"I will go to Australia with you, to your sheep ranch."

"Station. It's called a station," he said with growing frustration. "How do I convince you?"

"You cannot," she said smiling. "While you were asleep, I have been thinking of our options."

"Our options?"

"Yes, If not Switzerland, we go to Italy. I have been there with Andres. I know how to do it."

"We need to stop for the night. You look exhausted and I must consider a plan. Juliet, can you find us a pension?"

"I know where, Charles."

They stopped at a small pension called La Suisse.

"Two rooms for the night," Charlie said as if he needed an explanation. The young man nodded with a wry smile.

"No," she interrupted, stepping forward. "We are lovers, Charlie." She wrapped her arms around him. "One room only."

Charlie looked at her, frowning.

In their small room, Charlie turned to her. "Why did you tell him that?"

"So they understand and won't disturb us," she said directly. "They know how to handle such things. Now they won't talk to strangers about us."

"Smart," he said, agreeing to the arrangement.

They ate what they bought earlier at a small market. Juliet began to undress to only her panties. She wore no bra. He tried to give her privacy but still he noticed her standing near the bed. Slim but not overly so, her skin was olive and smooth, he saw.

She looked at him, not moving. "You try not to watch, but I still see you," she said proudly and without inhibition.

"I am a man, Juliet, and you are a very beautiful woman."

"Americans," she said. "So politely and gentlemanly."

"I'll sleep here on the floor. You take the bed."

"No, we share. Get used to it." She turned off the single lamp and crawled into the old bed. It squeaked. Charlie undressed. She saw the .32 as he stuck it under his pillow. Before coming to bed, he braced a chair under the doorknob.

"Good idea. I like a man who is ready for anything." She pulled back the sheet and waited for him.

"I think we need sleep," he said sliding in beside her. She immediately snuggled up to him, pressing her breasts into his chest.

"You are making sleep very difficult."

"I just need to feel the warmth of a man beside me. "Good night, Charlie Stanek." She closed her eyes but not before feeling, but only touching him. "That is good. You like me that way," she whispered. It is important for our long trip to Australia or wherever," she whispered in his ear but he was already asleep. She smiled and slept, unmoving from her position with her arms wrapped around him tightly.

Early the next morning, without incident, they departed the pension for Italy. The old Citroen growled but moved, and soon they were crossing the frontier into Italy. Mountain travel was slow going for the old vehicle. They took turns driving, not knowing where exactly they drove. Charlie hoped to get to Venice and a ship going east, but didn't think the car would make that long a drive.

Almost to the top, the old Citroen finally died, gasping and clanging for the final time. Charlie was driving and he pulled the car over, coasting to a stop along a steep ravine.

"Grab your bag, now we hitchhike," he said, standing along the road while Juliet sat behind him on a large rock. Traffic was light. The time passed without success.

"I will try," she said. The first action was to pull her skirt up to her thigh. She turned to Charlie and smiled. "Sometimes, my love, this will work."

Soon a late model Mercedes pulled over. He motioned for Juliet to come to the window.

"Where to?" he asked in heavily accented French. She told him that they were traveling to Milan.

"Get in," he said. With Juliet in front and Charlie in the back seat, they turned onto the highway and headed east down the mountain.

"Where do you go?" Juliet asked the man, who was about her age, muscular, with light hair and brown eyes. She thought him not very good looking as she scanned him closely. First impressions were everything to the young woman. Juliet immediately decided she trusted Charlie, no one else.

"I go to Roma for business," he replied. "I come from Paris where I live."

"I live there also," she said. "Where in Paris. Perhaps, monsieur, we are neighbors."

The man began to explain where in Paris he lived, but she told him she did not know the neighborhood. "Yes, I've lived there only a short while," he said, to quickly amend his story.

"Did you come from the provinces?"

"No, I came from Czechoslovakia."

Juliet looked at Charlie who immediately spoke to the man in Czech. "Where?" he asked. "In Prague?"

"Yes," the man replied in Czech. "I am a buyer of farm implements for the government."

"Important and very useful," Charlie replied. He wished he had not revealed that he spoke the language. With three languages used among them, the conversation grew interesting and lively by the time they reached the foothills and soon gliding into Italy's north plain. About an hour later, the Mercedes with its passengers entered a small village. "I must stop here for petrol," Urick, told them.

"Yes, thank you, Urick" Charlie said as they got out of the car. "We will spend the night here. It is a beautiful place."

Urick was surprised at his announcement.

Juliet looked at him, taken aback.

"Yes, it is so romantic and we can spend our time alone," she said, hugging Charlie. "Good bye Urick."

Walking down a short hill to the center of the village, Juliet spoke. "Why Charlie? He would take us all the way to Milano, I think."

"Something strange about him. I don't know what it is. He was very friendly, almost too friendly, I think," Charlie replied. "I learned that implement buyers operating in the West are often fronts for the KGB."

Juliet instinctively squeezed his hand. "Did I say too much?"

"No, but our plans have changed. We are not going to Milan."

"Charlie, something else."

"What?"

"That neighborhood—Place Maubert where he said he lives—is mostly Asian and poor, not for a European who can afford to drive a German Mercedes. Does he really live there or is that the only one he could name?"

"They've picked up our trail," he said worried.

"We will find a place to stay and talk more about it," she said.

"You are a good detective, I think." He stopped walking to kiss her on the cheek.

Later, in a small hotel she found. They talked, both in bed, she in her panties and Charlie had stripped down to his boxers. "Now, I feel free," she announced, peeling off her panties, not concerned about what Charlie may say. She had had enough of conversation, he easily saw. She began to rub his body slowly and passionately. "Are you tired tonight, my love," she asked, touching him softly and moving lower down to his thighs to slip her hands into the boxers, slowly sliding them off him.

He smiled, "Not tonight," he whispered and bent to kiss her breasts, touching each with his tongue. He forced Urick from his mind, and he quickly discovered, not with too much difficulty. He had learned long ago how to lock up his troubles and concerns.

She pushed his hands lower. "More, my love." Both naked, she guided his hands. He felt the damp warmth of her loins.

They made love until both were exhausted. Not wanting to let go of him, she held him tightly, her legs wrapped around his thighs. "Now we are lovers," she whispered, "and I will keep you right here even as we herd sheep. Feeling quenched, she soon fell off to sleep.

The next morning Charlie awoke, feeling pleasantly refreshed. He touched her thighs. She sleepily rolled over, placed a pillow under her breasts, and spread wide for him.

"Now my love," she murmured as if in a dream. She guided him into her.

"I think I love Americans," she said later as Charlie slowly rose from the bed to dress. "Even sheep herders."

He laughed, something he had not done in many days.

To avoid Milan, they took three trains to reach Venice through the Italian countryside. On the final leg of their journey, Charlie noticed a man—older, casually dressed and reading a newspaper. He was heavy, but not fat, muscular. He wore a fedora. He recognized him as someone he had seen on an earlier train. *They found us,* he thought, disturbed. *Urick.*

Arriving in Venice, Charlie stayed behind to follow the man. "I will meet you inside," he told Juliet. He had to ensure the man followed him. His new strategy depended on it.

The station was crowded and easy for Charlie to escape the man's sight. He stepped behind a small kiosk. The man walked by him. Juliet stood at a high table and Charlie saw that the man slowly walked by her without stopping. He looked around as if searching. Charlie knew he looked for him, so he accommodated him and emerged from behind the kiosk. Seeing him, the man then quickly stepped back into the crowd.

To watch me, Charlie decided.

Charlie went to Juliet's table. "We must find a hotel," he said loudly—too loud. "Come."

She saw that something was wrong.

Charlie said nothing more and they caught a taxi, directing the driver to a hotel. He knew the man watched them leave and would probably follow.

"They found us. I know," she said to him in the taxi.

At a small hotel, they checked in under Charles Klinehoff. In their room, Juliet watched Charlie but did not panic.

It seemed like a quiet, peaceful place. Too bad, he thought, paying for the room upfront. *I would have loved to see more of the city.*

"You will leave for another hotel while I stay here," he ordered her when they got to their room. "I am giving you money to go anywhere you desire. But you must wait until after dark. Take a back stairs. Do not let anyone see you."

He sat down and wrote a long letter on hotel stationary. Finished, he addressed the envelope to himself at his Outback address. "Mail this tomorrow, then leave Venice as quickly as you can. Do you understand?" he saw that she was frightened. He tried to smile. "Don't worry, they want me not you."

Darkness came to the city of canals. Too damn early, he thought. "It is time for you to go, my sweet Parisian, my lovely Juliet. I will never forget you," he said, sadness in his voice. "Now go. I will check the hallway."

She did, grabbing her bag with Charlie's letter, but not before one last kiss.

He checked that the hallway was clear and quiet.

"I will love you always," she said and was gone.

He missed her already. Juliet had made him feel alive and not caught in the tragic drama of his endless war. *Yes, she is free,* he thought, sad but relieved.

Charlie knew they would come for him, and he knew they would not wait while they had him in Venice. They had lost him too many times already. However, he did not know if they would try to kill or capture him. He pulled out the .32, checked it, and then left the room.

He easily found a hiding place in a linen closet near the room. He kneeled to wait, the door slightly ajar. The hours passed slowly. He thought of Juliet, hoping she was safe somewhere far from here.

Charlie closed his eyes so he could listen with all his senses. From his experiences in the Outback with Rusty, he had learned that it worked. He taught him during the long nights on the range, miles from the station. Now, bathed in deep darkness he watched, certain that evil would soon come.

The stairway steps creaked and groaned under the full weight of a man. Completely focused, Charlie followed him. With each step, the man grew closer. Charlie gripped the .32 tightly in his hand, the safety off. Suddenly, the footsteps were on the hardwood floor in the hallway near his room. One man, he heard.

Fools, if they believed one man would do it. Another must be close, in the lobby or car nearby, he decided. Charlie knew what he had to do, and timing was everything.

Without knocking, the man leaned into the door hard, crashing it open. He opened up with his automatic as he entered the room. He sprayed the bed with bullets. Charlie discerned that it was a Tokarev with silencer. Russian.

He made his move, silently but rapidly, to get behind the shooter.

"Drop it," he ordered in Russian. The man chose to turn on him instead, still with the weapon in his hand.

Charlie fired two rounds into the man's chest. They were loud cracks. The man stepped back but still held his pistol.

Charlie fired again, this time penetrating to the man's heart.

The man fell dead.

I have to get the hell out of here. He turned and ran for the exit door, down the backstairs and out.

Soon, sirens began to wail.

He walked and walked, hoping he was putting enough distance between himself, the cops, and the KGB. He figured everyone was looking for him. The police had his name, description, and the KGB knew he was loose in the city.

Nearing the dock, he had a flash of insight. He pulled out the "Charlie Klinehoff" passport. *I have to keep using it,* he thought. Charlie still had the other passport in his trousers, the one that said he was Charles Stanek, Major, United States Army. He knew he had to hold onto it, certain it would prove invaluable at some point.

He waited for sunrise and the opening of shops. He needed a complete change of clothing—hat and all.

Chapter 25

Charlie spent the remainder of the night walking and drinking coffee. The shops along the canals slowly opened at dawn. The sirens had quieted within minutes after his escape from the hotel, leaving him just another tourist late night walking the city.

He looked for an apparel store that could accommodate his needs. He found one not far from the great square in the heart of the city—San Marcos. He entered and began quickly shopping—a shirt, trousers, jacket, and finally, he saw the head covering he must have. It was a beret, much like the one Juliet wore. Hers had impressed him. It seemed to scream romance. He paid in cash, dressed in back, and soon was on his way.

Charlie sought out the docks. He decided he would sign on to the next ship leaving port. Freighter or passenger, it did not matter, but he knew a freighter was safer for him. He slowly made his way down the several piers inquiring about destination and schedules. He finally found a freighter loaded with steel products bound for Haifa, via Athens. The ship was scheduled to leave within hours.

Damn lucky, he thought, showing his passport to the ship's captain. The man looked at Charlie strangely. "Why Mr. Klinehoff? American, no?" he asked, but accepted his payment graciously.

"I do not like airplanes, and I think this is the best way to see the world."

"Ha! We shall see," the ship's captain replied.

"I want to see Israel."

The captain nodded. He had long ago learned not to ask too many questions of his passengers. "Welcome aboard the "Italian Princess," he said, pointing the way down a corridor to Charlie's cabin. "We depart in four hours. You may want to buy food for the journey. Not much to offer."

"I would prefer a berth on a lower floor, captain. If that's possible."

The captain sighed, and then nodded. "If that's what you want, I will prepare one near crew quarters."

"Yes, thank you." Charlie disembarked to shop. He mainly wanted to keep an eye on who else may yet travel aboard the Italian Princess.

He stood in a small market next to the dock where the ship tied up. He quickly grabbed items—bread, cheese, sliced salami, and beer—while keeping an eye on who boarded.

He saw only one older man come aboard who Charlie decided was not crew. The man, slightly stooped and very thin, carried a suitcase. Charlie was relieved. He thought he could handle one old man if it came to that.

On time, the Italian Princess embarked for Athens. Charlie stood at the rail near the bow. He watched as the old steamer slowly made way.

Juliet, where are you? he wondered. The thought of losing her made him feel sad and empty. With Truin, it was mostly about passion and longing, for the past that was gone and for a future that could never be. Juliet was different. Living in the moment. Charlie brooded, something he seldom did. He shrugged to force himself to put his memories of Juliet and Truin away. He hoped his son and Rusty received his letter and understood. Five months was a long time to be away.

He had to focus on the business of survival. The old man he had seen earlier approached him.

The sea journey to Athens was an uneventful two days. Passing Brindisi, Charlie learned the older man was traveling to Israel to visit his youngest daughter. He said his name was Roberto Rosenberg, and he operated a small business in Rome. He had survived the war by hiding with gentile friends and bribing local officials. Even then, the final round up by Nazis had claimed his two sons who he never saw again.

After the war ended, he placed his daughter on a ship bound for Palestine. "A new life for her," he told Charlie. "Maybe when I retire, I will go there also." His wife had died before the war. Charlie was relieved to learn that he and Roberto were the ship's only passengers to Athens. The captain had confirmed it.

Charlie chose to stay on board while docked at Athens' port. The food on the Princess, as meager as it was, was eatable. He stood at the starboard side watching for additional passengers.

He saw only one person come aboard. A younger man, dressed as a tourist walked slowly up the gangplank. Nothing indicated the man's identity or profession. *I'll have to keep an eye on him,* Charlie decided. Going below when the ship prepared to disembark, he quickly saw the man take a cabin next to his, a cheaper berth in the bowls of the ship. A poor tourist? He wondered.

He had not been carrying his weapon, but now decided he had to, at least until he could identify his new neighbor. The first day at sea, the man never left his cabin, not even for meals. Charlie, keeping watch, found that interesting. Late, on the second day, he decided it was time to introduce himself. He knew that was the only way he could control the situation.

Before presented with an opportunity to go next door...

The final night before they reached Israel the old freighter hit rough seas; a subtle rocking motion permeated the entire ship. Charlie lay in his bunk trying to sleep but finding it impossible. He heard a soft knock at the door. "Who is it?" he demanded in a loud voice.

"Your neighbor," answered the man. "I need to speak with you." He spoke in clear, American English.

"Sorry, tomorrow," he replied. "I was asleep."

"Only for a moment."

Charlie reached for the automatic, and then stepped softly to the door. "Wait a minute," he said. I can't take any chances. He flipped off the safety, holding the gun at his side as inconspicuously as he could yet ready for action.

He opened the door. "What do you...?"

Before he finished his question, An American Army .45 pointed at his head.

"Step back slowly, Major Stanek, and drop the weapon."

Charlie did as requested. The man, in a t-shirt and barefooted, looked around the cabin. "Move back and sit on the bunk," he ordered, kicking the .32 to the side, out of Charlie's reach.

Charlie again complied. He feverishly searched his head for a counter-move—anything that offered him an advantage.

"We know about you, Major. It seems that everyone in Europe from the radio traffic we are intercepting is looking for you and your woman. Where is she by the way?"

"Long gone. I gave her money and told her to get away, anywhere. She probably returned to Paris, but hell, I don't know. She knows nothing about me so forget her," he told the man.

The young man shrugged. "No matter."

"Who the hell are you? KGB?"

"He looked insulted. "Never." He did not loosen his grip on the weapon he held.

"If you plan to kill me, do it, damn it." Charlie saw that he could not move against him. He had him covered tight.

"Just want information."

"You didn't say who you are."

"Mossad, Israeli Institute of Intelligence and Special Operations."

"I must know your business traveling to my country," he demanded. "Whose side are you on, Major Stanek? That is not clear. Do you work for the Americans or the Soviets? Are you operating in Central Europe or Indochina? You live a very complicated life with both Americans and Soviets searching for you, as you seem to be traveling the world. Why?" I ask myself.

"I'm just an Australian sheep herder trying to get back home."

"Ha! Good story for a spy, but I'm not stupid," the young man said. "The ship's captain, an old friend, tells me a man meeting Stanek's description is onboard his ship, so I must investigate. Don't make this confusing. Talk."

In very general terms, omitting the details, he explained his mission to Saigon and his changed mission to Paris. "That was a disaster. The KGB tagged me before I even got off the plane from Washington," Charlie said. "Now, who the hell are you?"

"I already told you who I work for. The name is Josef Ezra Cantor, formerly of New York City."

Not tall, not short, but good looking in an urban sort of way. He had close-cropped blond hair, and his brown eyes burned into Charlie with an intensity that screamed, "Kill." "So, what are you going to do, Josef Cantor?"

Finally, Cantor lowered his weapon and smiled. But he never changed focus. His eyes never moved from Charlie. "From the sound of your story, you're waging your own private little war, Major. And alone, as I don't see where you're getting much help."

Charlie shrugged. "That seems to be how things are unfolding, but I always believe in the good guys who seem to appear when I most need them. That's something I learned fighting in World War Two with the partisans in Central Europe and later with the Vietnamese."

He shook his head. "I think you have a long journey ahead of you wherever you're going. In the meantime, if you stay in Israel, we'll have both the CIA and KGB breathing down our neck, you being such a popular guy."

"If you aren't going to shoot me, what?"

"Cantor sighed. "I can't help you much, but I can do one thing. I will arrange transportation for you to Bombay. Where you go from there is your business and not our concern as long as it isn't back here."

Chapter 26

Cantor kept his word and arranged passage for Charlie on a freighter bound for Asia. It was a long slow voyage but Charlie arrived in Bombay without incident. He believed the Mossad agent when he told him no one would ever know the two met on the Mediterranean, not even Cantor's superiors.

Charlie was amazed at all the changes he saw around him. In the eight years since he had passed through the region, a Jewish state and an India independent after a hundred years of British rule. He knew other colonized peoples soon would follow, whether through war like the Indochinese states or peacefully. Bombay bustled with several millions living there. Walking near the docks, the poverty he saw frightened him.

Earlier on the voyage across the Indian Ocean, he destroyed the Klinehoff passport and scattered the pieces to the wind. That done, he breathed a sigh of relief. The document helped him little in his mission in Europe.

He learned by chance that the freighter he traveled on was picking up a cargo of raw cotton destined for Singapore, then on to Melbourne for wool. *My wool*, he hoped, thinking again about the station, his son, and the drovers. Not an hour had passed without thinking of them. He book passage through to Australia, choosing to stay on "Blue Sky." Charlie had made this journey before, during his return from Europe in '48, so he was not a stranger to the exotic ports of South Asia.

Again, he watched closely as passengers embarked for the first leg of the voyage to Singapore. The gangplank filled with travelers, but he saw that they were mostly Indian nationals. The last time he made this trip, ex-servicemen returning home from the war filled the ship. Charlie easily stood out among the passengers. Then, so would any European-looking persons and that included Russian agents.

He hoped they had lost his trail in Europe, but he would never underestimate their reach. Charlie clearly remembered how they found him in central Australia in '48. Then they sent a messenger, very unsavory character, to retrieve me or kill me. "We have your woman and child," Pavlov wrote in a very cryptic note designed to bring him back to Czechoslovakia. He figured they would try again, and he knew he had to be prepared.

The voyage was uneventful until he reached Australia, the final destination. There he ran into difficulty passing through Australian customs at the Melbourne port of entry. The agent had trouble with Charlie's passport.

"Why does an officer in the United States Army travel on an old freighter?" the burly man with red hair and a permanent scowl asked, holding up the process. "You got on where? Saigon? The last stamp. Were you working there for your government?" he asked more bored than inquisitive.

"I decided to see more of Asia before returning to the States," Charlie told him.

The agent did not believe him. "Please sir, go sit there and I'll contact my superiors." Charlie obliged him. Soon, an Australian

Army officer approached. He held his passport. "Major Stanek, please come with me."

Charlie followed him into a large room off the customs area. Several soldiers stood near, all listened as the man began to question him. "Sir, we're not making much sense of your entry by freighter. Surely, a major in the United States Army can find better accommodations. Can you explain?"

Charlie told him he had spent time in Cambodia before taking the freighter. "I have been on an assignment deemed "Top Secret," and now on my way to the American Embassy in Canberra." He needed a good story. "After completing my mission to Indochina, the agency requested I travel to Phnom Penh to clear up an issue," he lied. Nondescript and vague, he hoped they would get the message that he was on an espionage assignment.

The agent called the U.S. embassy for verification. They spoke with Jon Grey. The process was slow. Finally, they got the message, and as Charlie represented a close ally of Australia, offered him passage on a military hop to their capitol. Charlie graciously accepted. It was now October—growing hot in Central Australia. Charlie had been away for almost seven months on a mission Grey had assured him would last several weeks at most.

Somewhere in the Indian Ocean, before Bombay, Charlie knew who murdered John Sawyer. It seemed so clear to him now. It had to have been an inside job, by someone inside Vietnam. He decided it was the Viet Minh, perhaps Truin, who made the decision to kill Sawyer. Yet she assured me in Saigon she had not given the order. Did she lie? Charlie quickly understood he would never know. They must have learned Sawyer planned to kill their top leadership, not a difficult deduction for me, but evidently, not one the CIA made. Truin had the means, at her hotel, and plenty of opportunities to order a subordinate to lace his food with poison.

No direct Chinese or Russian involvement as the Directorate had suspected. The CIA probably believed the Vietnamese lacked the skills or motivation to kill an American, so needed their assistance. Yet, from Quan and the Russian woman, the KGB knew I was in Vietnam. Why didn't they get me? Was I protected? Truin? Charlie considered that, too.

She protected me when they so easily could have captured me as they did in '45. Then they took me to Hanoi where Andre Pavlov waited to interrogate me. Only luck and another Russian saved me from a gulag. I guess Sawyer's killing will go down in history as a heart attack. Charlie shrugged, disgusted that he was ordered to go all the way to Europe to figure things out.

Americans and the Viet Minh are engaged in a war, but it is not my war, not anymore. When I return to my station near Alice Springs, I become a simple sheepherder again. Charlie was determined to stay out of a fight he knew was coming.

Before boarding the DC-3 for his ride to Canberra, he stopped at a newsstand. He saw the headlines from the *Los Angeles Times*. They screamed at him. "Diem Wins Election in South Vietnam with 90 percent of the vote to become President. National Elections scheduled for 1956 annulled with U.S. Support." He bought the paper, looked at the byline and saw that Betty McCarthy wrote the article. Charlie smiled. *Still doing her job*, he thought with a smile. Reading down, he learned that Diem had received 600,000 votes in Saigon even though only 450,000 registered to vote. *Of course*, he thought, now convinced that was their plan all along.

On the ride, he sketched out what he would say to Grey. The thought of meeting with him again turned his stomach. If I did not need a work visa here, I would have told Cantor to tell the world he shot me and threw me over into the Mediterranean.

I'd have figured a way to smuggle myself into the country, but with my son to think of, I could not take the risk. They would have learned the truth eventually but I would have bought some time. But to go where?

Chapter 27

"Neither the Russians nor Chinese appear to have much interest in what goes on in Saigon," Charlie told Grey in the small office in the American Embassy. "The killing was planned and executed by the Vietnamese. They must have learned Sawyer was tracking them."

Grey nodded, taking copious notes for his report to Washington. He looked up. "Washington had suspected as much, but they had to be certain. The Russians and the Chinese knew you were there—we made no secret of it—yet they made no attempt on your life."

Always the bureaucrat, Charlie thought, watching him. "As it turned out, the KGB was interested in getting me, but they failed. They tracked me from Washington, and then chased me through Western Europe. They don't give up easily, do they?"

"Sawyer made mistakes there, his cover too easily penetrated, but we had to know if the KGB still searched for you. Rosebud is that important to them and I don't think they like you all that much, Stanek. Revenge is probably another factor that Washington considered with their decision to send you to Europe."

"So they used me as bait, eh?"

"Don't look at it that way, Stanek. America thanks you for a job well done. And we have leads on their network we would not have had otherwise."

Charlie stared at him.

"The Russians desperately want to find Rosebud. Was her cover blown?"

"Assure them that Rosebud is alive and well. I didn't expose her identity," Charlie replied. "But Henry Eisenberg's cover is blown."

"We were willing to make that sacrifice, and we have other good contacts in London. MI6 will take care of things there."

"Grey, you bastard," Charlie growled. "You will never change, will you? The same Ivy League prick I found in Czechoslovakia. You had no intention of negotiating with Madame Thieu for Diem's replacement."

He chose to ignore the insult. "Washington was divided on that, Stanek. There were those wanting to remove him while others determined to stick with him. So your mission was valid."

"Thanks for the reassurance," he replied.

"And Madame Thieu? What has happened to her?"

"I don't know as no one has been assigned yet to Sawyer's mission, and intelligence is real sketchy on the Viet Minh cadre in the South."

That must mean she is safe...for the moment, he hoped. "John, Jack, whoever, was dispatched from here to assassinate the Viet Minh leadership in the south. Did that include her?"

Grey shrugged, still writing. "If it was necessary, he had approval to do it."

"My mission to Europe. It all seemed so believable."

"We had to know if their networks were operating in Indochina. Sending you got things jumping across the continent, and even in Saigon," he said. "Brilliant idea."

"Fuck you."

"It's a shame you had to kill their agent in Venice. We could have learned a few more things from him about Russian espionage activities," Grey said. "We've already notified our allies. They're tracking KGB contacts."

"You ID the dead agent?"

"Of course," he said. "Stanek, congrats on a job well done. I will write up my report and get it to Washington ASAP on the next hop. Your mission is accomplished." Grey stood, signaling to Charlie that the meeting was at an end.

"Wait, not so fast, Grey. I want my work visa and a fresh passport.

Grey looked at him and smiled. "I'll have them for you tomorrow. Hell Stanek, I'll even get you a plane to Alice Springs."

The whole damn world now knows where I reside. Hell, this prick will probably come for a visit, Charlie thought, standing. "I'll be here bright and early for my visa and new passport."

The plane was a small Cessna but it beat hitching. An older man Charlie knew from his few visits to Alice Springs even offered to fly him out to Russel Station for a fee. The ride was long with the man not a talker and Charlie too excited. He touched down on an open field near the barns.

His field hands waved to him as he disembarked the small plane, but Charlie had to first greet his son. He walked, ran up to the homestead. "Georgie! Georgie! Where's my boy?" he called, jumping onto the front porch. He saw a light in the kitchen and knew someone was home.

"Daddy! Daddy!" he heard. A small figure raced through the front room, out the screen door, and into Charlie's arms. They hugged. Tears filled his eyes.

"My boy let me look at you." He admired the child, spinning him, and then tickling him.

George laughed and jumped back into his arms.

"I'll never leave you again," he whispered, still tearful.

Another figure walked through the front room following George. Charlie looked up surprised, and smiled as a young woman approached. She wore his old, heavily stained Stetson. One of his shirts hung from her, but she had neatly tied it around her waist. A pair of jeans, cut-off high on her thighs revealed tanned legs. She marched through the house as if she belonged.

"I knew you'd get back," she said, "No Russian could ever stop Charles Stanek."

"Juliet," he said beaming. "I thought you returned to Paris." He reached out to her and soon all three were embracing. "How did you know I'd return?"

"Rusty said your spirit is strong and protects you from evil. He said that soon you would return to us. I believed him."

Charlie smiled. "You traveled all this way. I think your spirit is stronger than mine."

"I had to see your sheep," she replied, smiling. They embraced and then kissed, long and passionately.

THE END

We hope you have enjoyed reading Robert Tecklenburg's *Charlie Stanek's War*. If you have not had the opportunity to read his other titles with BluewaterPress LLC, may we suggest his novel, *Prague: Darkness Descending*, and *The Last Mission*. Both are available online through bluewaterpress.com.